Just Within a Highland Mist

A Highland Gardens Novella
The 5th tale in the series.

Dawn Marie Hamilton

ISBN: 978-0-989964289

*This novella is dedicated
to those who dare to dream.*

ACKNOWLEDGMENTS

So many individuals helped bring this book to fruition. Too many to mention here, but you know who you are, and I hope know you have my heartfelt thanks.

Thank you to Cindy Davis for editorial guidance. To Cathy MacRae for planting the seed that inspired Tevin's time traveling adventure and for critiques. And to Cate Parke for critiques. Words cannot convey how important you are to me.

Thank you to Frank, my husband, best friend, and personal hero.

Most importantly, thank you to the readers of the Highland Gardens series.

CHAPTER ONE

Present day
North Carolina

Mist snaked over the hills and vales of the Blue Ridge Mountains settling on the Village of Anderson Creek and surrounding woods like a shroud. Emily stumbled through ever-thickening fog, trying to avoid the slap of tree branches obscured by vaporous wisps, fear pressing against a constricted chest. How had she lost the boys?

Malcolm was too bold for a seven-year-old, and the year younger Tevin followed his adopted brother into every unfortunate escapade. She'd only turned away for a moment to check her smart phone for a signal—a nonexistent signal—and the boys jumped upon the opportunity to bolt through the woods, brandishing wooden swords more than likely against the beast they claimed to track—an orange dragon.

"Life or death!"

The Clan MacLachlan battle cry spat in the distance from the children's lips hung heavy on the humid air.

Emily raced in the direction she believed the bellow came from and tripped over a root, losing balance. "Dammit to hell." She slipped on decaying leaves and banged an elbow on the trunk of a tree; the jolt of shock lit up her nervous system. "Ouch, ouch, ouch!" She danced around and shook out her tingling arm, then taking a moment to regain composure, leaned her forehead against the rough bark of the old oak and inhaled a deep calming breath. "Please let me find the boys."

Jillian and Stephen MacEwen would never forgive her if anything happened to their sons while she babysat them. The sharp snap of a twig sent her off in an altogether different direction. How had the walk from the inn to the MacEwen's log cabin become such a nightmare? Normally, Emily knew the way through the woods to and from the MacLachlan and MacEwen homes, *Foxgloves* garden center, and the *Whispering Pines Inn*, but the fog made everything appear different— menacing.

Stopping to catch her breath, she scanned the immediate surroundings. Unable to discern a path, she chewed on a chapped lip. To where had the boys run?

"Malcolm! Tev! Where are you?" she called into the fog.

Tevin's little-boy shriek jammed her heart into her throat. She sprinted in the direction of the frightening screech, ignoring the sting of branches grazing her face as she darted past haunting tree after tree.

She slid to a stop at the base of the forbidden mound just beyond the garden gate of *Foxglove's* display garden. Like with the eye of a storm, no mist encroached upon the knoll. Malcolm stood at the far edge, to the side of the mound, feet apart, wooden sword held forward in two firm hands, tip pointed toward Tevin, whose feet were planted on the hilltop in a wide stance, sword held in a similar manner although *his* hands trembled. Emily had been warned numerous times by Iain MacLachlan, chief of the local branch of Clan MacLachlan and her boss at the inn, to never, ever, not under any circumstance, step foot onto the mound. And certainly she wasn't to permit any of the MacLachlan or MacEwen children in her care to go there. She'd never understood why.

Never asked why. Had thought the warning silly.

Dread stole her breath and she inhaled sharply. "Tevin, come here."

"I don't want to go away and fight the dragon alone," he groused.

"It's okay, Tev," she said. His profile seemed like a black and white photograph in the fog with his damp hair curled against a pale face. The precocious boy had wheedled a special place in her heart, and was a favorite among the children, although she tried not to show too much favoritism. "You don't have to fight dragons. Come with me. We'll cut through the garden to Laurie and Patrick's house. I bet your cousins have hot chocolate."

Tevin didn't move, didn't say anything, didn't look at her. He kept a level stare on his brother.

"Malcolm, tell him to come to me."

"No. He's on a quest to kill a dragon."

"Oh, for pity sake. Enough of this." She'd just drag him off. Patience gone, Emily stepped toward the mound and encountered some sort of barrier. She pressed a finger into it and released. *Snap.* The obstruction seemed to be made of clear...plastic wrap? She moved to the right and then to the left, but the barrier remained. She couldn't get through it, as if the mound was encased in a clear plastic bubble. None of this made sense.

How did Tevin get through if she couldn't?

She glanced over a shoulder. Across the garden, lights brightened the windows of the MacLachlan family's house on one end, and the garden center's gift shop at the other, but neither building was close enough that anyone inside would hear a call for help. She glanced at her phone. Halleluiah! She had a signal. Without removing her gaze from Tevin, she rang the house phone. The phone rang and rang. No answer.

Hu...hu-hooooo. The eerie call of a barred owl grated on already raw nerves.

"Please, Tev, please come here," she said. He ignored her. There must be a way to get him through the barrier.

3

Perhaps his mother was still at the garden center even though it should have closed an hour ago. Emily rang the number for the gift shop. "Oh, thank God. Jillian, I'm with the boys in the woods near the mound. We got lost. The fog is so thick. I lost the boys. Then I found them. I can't get Tevin to come to me. He's on the mound just beyond the garden gate. Some sort of…oh, I don't know…barrier is keeping me from going to him. I don't know what to do." *Dammit. I'm rambling.*

The, "Oh, shit," coming from the phone's tinny speaker confirmed her fears, and ratcheted up the angst curdling in her stomach.

"Tev, your mom's on the phone. Come talk to her. Pah-lease."

He touched her with his gaze, shook his head, blue eyes solemn, damp blond curls stuck to cherub cheeks.

Suddenly, tiny sparkling lights flashed about, darting to and fro, settling high in the branches of the one tree on the mound—a beautiful sight. Tevin looked up. His eyes widened in amazement. And…and the little boy vanished.

August, 1521
Fir-wood, Scottish Highlands

A snagged thread in the fabric of time sent a ripple through the earth realm felt only by those sensitive to such things. Munn stopped in his tracks and perked a pointed ear. Did he hear the murmuring of a new changeling in the wood?

He desperately wished to ignore the woeful sound, but something unbeknownst to him drew him to the *bairn*. He whirled onto the *Sìthichean Sluaigh*, the knoll of the Fae, spinning in circles, sucking last year's fallen leaves into the whirlwind propelling him until he slowed to a stop.

This wee male was different than the other *bairns* of the wood. Dressed different. Cleaner. Munn scratched a whiskered chin. He should flee. Not get involved.

The blond lad stood. Stared with narrowed eyes. "Munn?"

"How do you ken my name?" He'd never seen this lad afore.

The *bairn* sniffled and wiped his nose on the sleeve of his tunic. "My cousin Allison tells stories about you. You're the Clan MacLachlan brownie. Your duty is to watch over the clan."

Munn puffed out his chest. *I am legendary.*

"You look just like Allison said." The lad canted his head to the side. "You've pointy green boots, pointed ears, and a pointed green cap. You even have a scrunched brown face with whiskers."

"Humph." Munn frowned. "What be your name, lad? Who be your father?"

"Tevin." The *bairn* raised his chin. His gaze direct for one so wee. "My name is Tevin. My father is Stephen. Stephen MacEwen. He wouldn't want you to hurt me."

"Stephen's son?" *For Danu's sake.*

The wee time traveler nodded.

"Nary a one will harm you be you in my care," Munn said. "Where is your father?"

"I'm alone." Tevin squatted and picked up a wooden practice sword perhaps dropped upon arrival. He sliced the blade through the air. "Is this ancient Scotland? I'm on a quest to slay a dragon."

"Ach. A dragon you say?" Munn dithered. Should he impart the *bairn's* whereabouts? Might frighten the lad to ken he'd traveled through time. What should Munn do with the lad? Stephen would want him to protect his son. 'Twas obvious the *Sithichean* were involved in this mischief. But why would the Fae guide a *bairn* from the future to the past? "You are in Scotland, but not ancient Scotland. There are nae dragons here. By the bye, how did you get here?"

"My brother, Malcolm, pushed me onto the faerie hill and I traveled back through time." The *bairn* pursed his lips. "I guess not far enough."

Maclay? Damn that villain and his spawn. Even in death, Maclay was a boil upon Clan MacLachlan. Munn kenned the man's *bairn* would come to nae good. Stephen should never have championed the lad after his father's death and raised him as his own. Still…one of the Fae must be involved for the magic of the faerie hill to thrust a being through time. Especially such a wee being.

"Are you sure there aren't any dragons? He's orange," Tevin persisted.

Munn jerked his gaze to the *bairn*, annoyed by the interruption to his deliberation. He hated the need to think, but he must figure out what to do about the lad. "Who's orange?"

"The dragon. It is my destiny to slay the orange dragon."

"I told you. There are nae dragons here."

"But Allison and Malcolm said—"

Munn held up a hand. "You best forget about dragons and come with me to Castle Lachlan. The chief will ken what to do with you. And I dinnae want to hear any more about the winged beasts."

Tevin rolled his eyes to the side and curved tight lips into a disgruntled frown, but when Munn started off, the lad fell into step behind him. "What about the little faeries that brought me here? They have wings."

Munn stopped short, and the *bairn* slammed into his back. He spun around and righted the lad. "What faeries?"

"I thought they were dragonflies at first, but they're really cool. They're girls with wings. They brought me here. There was one with green wings and another with purple and—"

"Whist! Needs be I think."

Pixies? Why were pixies sifting time? What mischief did the ebony-haired Marcail and her pesky clan ponder?"

Present Day
Anderson Creek, NC

Emily gaped at the empty mound. "Where did Tevin go?"

"Don't know." Malcolm's darting gaze made her stomach drop to her knees. She hurried around the edge of the knoll to where he stood, a smirk on his face. He knew more than he'd admit.

"Yes you do. Your mom is on the way. She'll want to know where your brother went. Tell me where he is hiding before she gets here. Once we find him, we can go home."

"No!" He slammed two palms against her chest and shoved hard.

She propelled backward through the barrier as if it was nothing more than a bubble of soap. The cell phone flew from her hand, and she landed on her butt, the moist grass of the mound seeping through her leggings. "You little brat!"

Wow. He'd always been a handful, but she'd never called Malcolm a brat before. *Shit.* He seemed hostile—dark. The look in his eyes almost maniacal.

She pushed her palms against the ground to rise, but hesitated. Little sparkling lights flitted about her. Like lighting bugs. No—

Larger. Dragonflies? Perhaps—

Tee teehee hee. Tee teehee hee. Tee teehee hee. Feminine voices surrounded her with tinkling giggles.

"Who's there?" Emily's voice cracked. She leapt to her feet and whirled about, but didn't see anyone other than the gloating Malcolm.

Then everything went crazy. Spun. Or was she spinning?

She placed a hand on her stomach as if it was possible to hold nausea at bay. The ground fell out from beneath her. A scream caught in a suddenly parched throat. She plummeted downward into nothingness. Down...down...down, she dropped. What the—

A sonic boom made her head throb. She slapped her hands over ringing ears.

Something pulled her horizontally toward a bright white light. What was there? *Who* was there? She wished she could backpedal. The light burst like fireworks into bright colors. Red, orange, yellow, green, blue, indigo and violet—the colors of the rainbow.

Emily's vision dulled to gray then went black.

CHAPTER TWO

August 1521
Strathlachlan, Scotland

"Good luck to ye, lads." The blacksmith waved a broad hand.

Gregor returned the gesture then rocked forward in the saddle, prompting his horse to follow Duncan's lead. Two ghillies traveled with them, pack horses in tow for transporting the deer back to the castle.

They climbed the heather-covered incline behind the stables and forge as rays of sun peeked above the eastern ridge, painting the sky in shades of red and gold. The soft mossy scent of crushed purple blooms triggered fond memories of romping across the same slope when he fostered at Castle Lachlan as a green lad. Although his older brothers advised against returning to Strathlachlan due to rumors of fae activity, accepting a position as part of Archibald's *lèine-chneas* would prove the right decision. Serving under the ginger-headed Duncan, the captain of the MacLachlan chief's elite bodyguard, was an honor.

Besides, brownies and faeries didn't scare Gregor.

After riding along the ridge for a distance, they entered the wood and traveled a good path in single file with little chatter until the sun was high in the sky. Finally, Duncan raised a hand, halting them. Deer tracks crisscrossed the path.

Duncan grinned. "A small herd has crossed here."

Gregor slid from his horse and squatted. He fingered a deep track in the mud. "Fresh. Appears they've recently used this game trail."

Slim cuts bisected thickets on both sides of the path they'd been following, marking a much-used game trail.

"Me and Gregor will continue on foot. Secure the horses here and await our signal," Duncan instructed the ghillies.

After tying his mount to a tree near some fresh grass for grazing, Gregor slung his bow and quiver over a shoulder. He and Duncan followed the game trail for a distance in silence. 'Twas evident from the tracks a large stag travelled with the herd. His stomach bubbled with anticipation. A successful hunt would be the first deed in which he proved his worth to the clan.

The trail led them from the wood into a large clearing bordered by a semicircle of mountains. They climbed into the *corrie*.

"Keep low. Move slow," Duncan whispered, voice rough from exertion.

They found a herd of about fifteen hind and a large stag, and stalked within two hundred yards, but the wind direction changed and the animals spooked. Gregor and Duncan climbed onto the shoulder of the hill where they could move undetected. Clouds collided, darkening the sky.

"We have lost them," Duncan grumbled.

They retreated down the slope to the edge of the wood a substantial distance from the original game trail.

"Here." Gregor pointed at the ground and squatted. "This track is verra fresh. 'Tis the print of a single large stag."

"Ach, then, I will circle round. Flush him out for you."

They entered the wood together. Gregor found a decent spot behind a large boulder at the edge of a wee clearing from which to wait. He used two fingers to signal to Duncan he was in place, and the man disappeared through the trees. Time seemed to drag. He prepared the bow and selected the arrow with the straightest shaft from the quiver at his side.

Suddenly a hart wandered from the brush twenty-five yards upwind of Gregor's spot. The animal hesitated for a moment, mobile ears listening, sensitive nostrils testing odors in the air, then lowered his head and nibbled the tip of a leafy branch. Not just any hart, but a sixteen-point white stag—a mystical beast. Could the animal be real? Gregor closed his eyes; rubbed them. When he looked again, the animal was still there, browsing.

Breath quickened; excitement fired his blood.

He slowly, very quietly, raised his bow and nocked the arrow, praying he wouldn't spook the deer. The stag raised his head, ears perked. Eyes on the mark, Gregor drew the arrow steadily back until his right forefinger touched *the spot* on his jaw perpendicular to his right eye. He glanced along the length of the shaft, his aim perfect.

A lavender-winged dragonfly landed on the spine of the arrow just behind the hand that held the grip. One with iridescent green wings landed forward of the handgrip. A third buzzed his ear.

Lips curving into an annoyed frown, Gregor held the bow and arrow with one hand and shooed the bugs away with a wave of the other. His luck held. The deer continued to feed. As he prepared a second time for a clear shot, one of the bugs returned and perched on the arrow again. Stuck its tongue out at him. He jutted his head forward to better inspect the—

The bothersome creature stood on wee feet. Nae. Couldn't be. *She* had wee feet, wee arms and hands, and a curvaceous body draped in an iridescent purple fabric the same color that outlined her lavender diaphanous wings. She raised a dainty hand and tucked an ebony tress behind a pointed ear and smiled at him with rosy lips.

"What trickery is this?" he demanded.

Tee teehee hee, the pixie tinkled like delicate chimes.

The stag skittered, bounded over a thicket, and dashed into a copse of trees.

"Shite!" Gregor burst into a sprint without giving the pixies another thought, following the rustle of fallen leaves. The beast darted hither and farther, leapt barriers, doubled back on his tracks, and led Gregor on a merry chase. Gregor's muscles tired, but he kept going until he completely lost all trace of the animal. How much distance had he traveled? For how long? He couldn't guess. When had the heavy mist crept over the land?

He sucked in much-needed air as he slumped against a tree and closed weary eyes. Disappointment a deep wound. The smell of damp earth combined with old fallen leaves and the rich scent of fir surrounded him. When he opened his eyes, he caught sight of a clump of coarse white hair stuck within the rough bark. The stag had come this way.

Perhaps I'll get another chance at the beast. Buoyed by the thought, he stalked through the fog-laden wood. As evening fell, he stole from the trees at the edge of a mist-free grassy mound. A bright full moon hung from the sky. The white stag, head held high, stood at the top of the knoll beside an ancient tree. Silvery lights sparkled in the branches like evening stars.

The deer caught sight of Gregor and stared with curiosity through lustrous brown eyes. He didn't spook, didn't run.

This was it. This would be Gregor's first kill since returning to Castle Lachlan. His heart beat too fast. He inhaled sharply, trying to steady his breathing. Instinctively, he rose to his full height, placed his feet at shoulder width, nocked the arrow, raised the bow, and drew the string back to his jaw. Aimed and...paused. Seemed wrong to kill such a magnificent beast.

The lavender pixie reappeared, jounced on the arrow, and blew dust into his face, startling an unintended shot from the bow. The white stag vanished as if it never existed. Standing in his place was a wide-eyed lass.

"Nae," Gregor howled. Shock and fear wrenched his gut.

He bounded onto the knoll. Thankfully, the wild shot had buzzed over the woman's shoulder barely grazing her ear. He slid to a stop in front of her. "By the Saints, what mischief is this?"

The woman met his gaze with the bluest of eyes and stole his heart in that moment. Then those beautiful eyes rolled back into her head, and she crumbled to the ground in a faint at his feet.

What should he do? He rubbed a niggling twinge over his heart, certain he'd just met destiny. 'Twas an uncanny fate such an eve'n be charged by magic. He knelt on one knee and gently brushed a lock of light brown hair away from the soft skin of her cheek sadly marred by scratches. He frowned, grasped the lass by the shoulders and shook. Her head lolled to the side, but she didn't waken.

"We have tracked you the better part of the afternoon and into the eve'n. What brought you to the *Sithichean Sluaigh?*" Duncan's deep voice startled him, as the man approached from behind. "Come, Gregor. Hurry. We must be away from this place of enchantment."

Gregor set aside his bow and lifted the woman into his arms. She was as light as a *bairn*. He stood, and turned toward his captain. "This is a faerie hill? That explains much."

"Aye. A knoll of the Fae." Duncan shivered then picked up the castoff bow. "Who have you found?"

"I dinnae ken." Gregor glanced at the ghillies and horses at the edge of the knoll. "She swooned."

"At the sight of you, aye?"

"Aye...*nae!*" He shook his head. How was he to explain the magic of this day? "We must take her to the castle for tending."

"Must we?" Duncan raised a brow. "We should set camp away from this place of enchantment and continue the hunt on the morrow."

"She is injured." Gregor held the man's stare.

Duncan's brow furrowed as he peered at the lass. "It appears naught but a flesh wound."

13

"Still…" Gregor had no intention of leaving the lass behind. Alone. Unprotected.

The big man's sigh resonated from deep within his chest. "Of course, we must take her to the castle," he finally yielded. "Lady Isobell will ken what to do."

The captain strode to the horses. With the lass cradled in his arms, head resting upon his shoulder, Gregor followed. She smelled sweet. Like flowers and summertime. Of days of happiness.

"She rides with me." He handed her to Duncan and mounted his horse.

The man's lips quirked when he lifted the lass and placed her in front of Gregor. "As you wish."

One ghillie rode in front, one to the rear, both holding torches raised high. The mist seemed to dissolve from around them. Where the trail widened, Duncan rode alongside.

"Will you tell me what happened back there?"

"I believe you flushed a white stag my way."

"Ah, the mystical beast believed to be a messenger from the otherworld. An encounter with a white stag is said to portend profound change in one's life." The man's gaze flicked to the lass for a moment.

"There is more," Gregor said.

"Then tell the rest."

"I waited where you left me behind the boulder in the wood. The white stag appeared and I readied my shot. What I thought were dragonflies landed on the shaft of my arrow. I believe they were pixies. Annoying wee sprites. They caused me to startle the stag, and he ran off."

Duncan's jaw tightened, but he said naught.

"You dinnae seem surprised."

"I am not."

"You believe in such things then?"

"Aye. And more."

"I chased the animal. Time seemed to…languish. The next thing I kenned was the beast on the faerie hill, then vanishing, and the lass…" Gregor gazed at the comely woman enwrapped within his arms. "Appeared as if by magic."

"A similar event happened here near to ten years ago."

"Do tell."

"Our chief's twin brother, Patrick, found a lass on the knoll after seeing her in visions."

Gregor swallowed uneasily. Some of his MacLachlan kin were known to have the sight. Mostly women, but occasionally men were born with the *gift*.

As a youth, Gregor kenned Patrick. The man had been an impressive warrior. A hero to Gregor. Years later, mystery shrouded the events leading to Patrick stepping down from the position of clan chief, naming Archibald, his twin brother, chief, and moving with his new wife to France. With time, rumors surfaced. Subtle at first then more insistent. Conjecture that they hadn't gone to France at all, but had traveled farther abroad—as in to another realm—to live amongst the Fae in faerie land.

A preposterous notion. Or was it?

He inhaled the scent of the woman in his arms. Foreign. Enticing. Enchanting.

"I almost shot the lass with a wayward arrow when one of the pixies startled me," he said.

Duncan snorted. "'Tis said they are particularly pesky."

Gregor tightened his hold on the lass, feeling an intense need to provide for her, to offer protection. "Who is she? Do you think she might be one of the Fae?"

"Nae. If she were, you would already be enchanted."

He squirmed and glanced at Duncan. Had the man read his mind? Gregor had become enchanted at first sight.

Deep in thought, he was surprised when the small hunting party broke from the wood onto the ridge above the stables and forge. Loch Fyne and Castle Lachlan lay below. Torchlight, leading from the distant beach to the castle situated on the islet within the small bay, shimmered on the calm water.

Trepidation slid into his gut. He'd intended to impress the

clan with his hunting prowess. Instead, he returned with an unknown lass.

By all that is Holy, what am I doing? The chief and his lady-wife might well be furious. And rightly so. What if I carry a Fae woman through their gate?

CHAPTER THREE

*D*own the slope from the stables, at the edge of the loch, across the bay from Castle Lachlan, Munn was losing patience with the lad in his care. "Stop draggin' your feet."

"When will we get there?" Tevin whined. "I'm tired and hungry."

I should have left the whelp in the wood to fend for himself, and forgotten he existed. Sweat broke out on Munn's skin with the spiteful thought. Stephen would be unforgiving if anything untoward happened to his son.

"Almost there," Munn said to appease the lad. "The castle is but a stone's toss across the bay."

"Oh. Wow." Tevin scuttled to the water's edge. "How will we get there?"

"In one of these." Munn dragged a *currach* across the shingle.

"Way cool."

"Actually, 'tis a warm eve'n."

The lad pursed his lips and scrunched his face as if he didn't understand the common fact. "But I—"

"Dinnae dawdle," Munn insisted. "Climb in."

Tevin did as told, sliding to the fore. Water lapped the small boat made of skins and wicker, making it bob up and down, and the lad gripped the gunwales on both sides. Munn pushed the craft farther into the water and jumped aboard, getting wet feet for his effort.

He sneezed then glared at the *bairn*. 'Twould be the lad's fault if Munn caught the grippe. It definitely wasn't the briny sea air irritating his nostrils. Stephen's son should have stayed in the future where he belonged.

Munn worried his fingers on his *trews*. The pixie clan were the most notorious and mischievous of the Fae. Why had they singled out the wee lad for an adventure?

He shook his head and took to the oars with a grumble. He hated the necessity to travel like a human. 'Twas easier to fade into the vanishing and travel on the breeze.

As they neared the castle beach, a horn blasted from the watchtower warning the castle folk of their approach.

"Wow. Look up there." Tevin sprang to his feet and pointed toward the battlements. The boat rocked precariously. "Those men have bows and arrows."

"Sit. Now," Munn said. "If you tumble into the frigid water, I will not suffer a dunking to fetch you."

The lad plopped onto his arse, but not before brackish water slopped over the side of the boat, dousing Munn's feet yet again. He mumbled a curse under his breath too foul for the ears of a *bairn*.

When the craft hit the shoal, Munn jumped into the shallow water. No point in trying to keep his feet dry at this juncture. He dragged the *currach* onto the shingle and...stilled. His sensitive ears perked. "Come out. I ken you hide behind the boulders, Lach."

The chief's son, Lachlan, poked his head from his hiding place with a frown. "How did you ken I was there?" He pointed at Tevin. "Who is he?"

"Cousin." Munn chose to ignore the first question. He wasn't about to share secrets with the lad. "Here for a visit."

Lachlan approached Tevin, and each lad studied the other.

The young MacLachlan lad fisted hands on hips. A mere couple of summers older than Tevin, the *bairns* were as different as night and day. Like his mother, Lachlan possessed the straight black hair and near purple eyes of his maternal Lamont forebears. Whereas Tevin, like his father, had the blond curls and light blue eyes of the majority of MacEwens, cousins to the MacLachlans.

At the sound of boots crunching gravel, Munn glanced away from the lads. Archibald strode along the path toward them, his gaze landing on his son with censure. "Your ma is searching the keep for you." He shifted attention to Munn and his charge, and raised a questioning brow. "Who have you brought to us?"

"Stephen's son, Tevin." Munn took a deep breath and huffed; answering so many questions was becoming a bore. "Found the *bairn* on the *Sithichean Sluaigh*. Alone."

"Indeed." The chief squatted in front of Tevin, lowered to the lad's height, and reached out an arm. "Welcome to Castle Lachlan, lad. I am—"

"I know who you are." Tevin grasped the offered arm as a warrior would, and shook. "You're Allison's Uncle Archie. You look just like Uncle Patrick."

Such a clever *bairn*. Munn rolled his eyes.

"Ach, well, we are twins, which in the same way as Patrick makes me your uncle, too." Archibald grinned. "What brings you to our gates?"

"He claims—"

"Let the lad answer, wee man."

Munn pursed his lips at the setdown, but kept his own counsel.

Tevin scraped a foot over the pebbles, his gaze following its path. Then he looked directly at Archibald and with all seriousness said, "I'm on a quest to slay a dragon."

"A noble endeavor…"

The *bairn* shot a triumphant smirk at Munn.

"Howbeit, I fear dragons nae longer exist," Archibald continued, deflating the lad's enthusiasm. "Perhaps you might tell me how you came to be here."

Tevin's shoulders sagged. "This isn't ancient Scotland?"

"I told you it was not," Munn interjected.

"Whist, *brùnaidh!*" the chief scolded for no good reason.

"Allison told us the faerie hill would take us to the land of dragons in ancient Scotland," Tevin said.

Lachlan edged closer, eyes wide, curiosity piqued.

"Malcolm said I had to go alone 'cause I need to prove I'm a man," Stephen's son continued.

Archibald's angry gaze shot to Munn, though he quickly blanked his features more than likely for the lad's sake.

Tevin sniffled as if holding back tears. "I didn't want to go by myself, but he pushed me onto the hill. Then the tiny faeries came and—"

The warning horn sounded a series of short blasts.

"Ach, the hunting party returns." Archibald stood. "Lachlan, take our guest to the kitchen and ask cook for bread with honey. Our lad here must be hungry from his journey."

"Come on." More curious than prudent, Lach waved an arm toward the keep, and Tevin followed, slowing to glance back once then hurrying to catch up to the older lad.

Archibald watched the two *bairns* scamper up the path to the courtyard before turning a scowl on Munn. "Is the Malcolm of which he spoke Maclay's son?"

"Aye."

"I worried when Stephen took in the orphaned *bairn*. 'Twas a chance, as a spawn of that villain Maclay, the lad would have troublesome tendencies. What a fine mess."

"Ach, a fine mess," Munn agreed, wholeheartedly.

"Is the fae Caitrina now meddling with the lives of *bairns?*" the chief asked.

"Nae." Munn swallowed uneasily. Caitrina, the halfling princess who lived amongst the humans in the future posing as a garden designer and part owner of the Foxgloves garden center in a place called Anderson Creek, was notorious for meddling with Highlanders' lives by using the faerie hill to sift time and for uniting unlikely lovers across the centuries. Though he strongly doubted her involvement with Stephen's son. "Lad claims to have been assisted through time by wee faeries. Pixies."

"Great. Just great." Archibald smacked a fist against his thigh. "When did pixies return to our soil? Why did you not advise me?"

"Did not ken of their reappearance until now."

"Can you summon Caitrina to take the lad home?"

"Nae. She has been in hiding for these past several years." *Ha. Hiding from an unwanted bridegroom, more than likely. What goes 'round—*

"Why?" Archibald waved a hand and shook his head. "Never mind. Not my concern. How will *we* return the lad home?"

Munn shrugged, having no answer for his chief.

The scraping of boats across shingle signaled the arrival from the mainland of the hunting party.

While the others retrieved the gear from the *currachs*, Gregor carefully debarked as not to jar the lass in his arms. Concern she had yet to awaken from her faint wrinkled his brow. He prayed Lady Isobell, the chief's wife, kenned how to rouse the woman.

"Dinnae see any bagged deer." Archibald strode toward them, a scowl engraved on his face. "Was the hunt a failure then?"

Gregor stiffened, taking the barb personally. But he had done right to abandon the hunt and bring the lass to Castle Lachlan for care. The chief would surely recognize the wisdom of such a course.

"We ran into mischief in the Fir-wood," Duncan said.

The chief raised an annoyed gaze to the man then shifted scrutiny to Gregor and the lass.

"Indeed." Archibald stepped in front of Gregor and brushed hair from the woman's face. "Emily?"

Gregor stiffened. He didn't care for the man touching *his* woman. *Shite!* "What?" He raised his gaze to Archibald. "You ken the lass?"

"Take her inside to Isobell. She will care for the girl."

How did the chief ken the lass? Gregor wanted an answer, but it was more important to get her out of the raw elements and tended to by someone who kenned what to do for her. He headed for the path toward the castle gate.

"Lad?"

Not more than three steps had he taken when the chief's bark halted him in place. "Aye?"

"Dinnae linger. Leave the lass with Isobell and her woman then report directly to my private chamber. I wish to have words with you."

"As you please."

When he entered the great hall, Lady Isobell rose from the table where she sat with one of her sons and another wee lad, a stranger, and hurried to his side. "Who have we here? Oh, my. Emily."

"You ken who she is?"

"Aye. Come with me." She marched across the stone floor, collecting her woman, Aine, along the way to the stairs. They ascended to the next level, and he followed them up the circular steps careful not to bang the lass's head against the hard stone wall, and along the passageway to a bedchamber decorated to a female's taste.

Aine directed him to the green velvet curtained bed, where he carefully placed the lass—*Emily*—among plump pillows and feather and fur bedding. The women fussed over her and shooed him away. He hesitated at the doorway, wishing to be of help. But the chief waited on him.

"Go," Lady Isobell instructed. "You must have tasks elsewhere."

Gregor nodded respectfully and reluctantly departed. He returned to the lower level of the keep and found Munn leaning against the gray stone wall beside the closed door of the chief's study. On Gregor's approach, the annoying wee man moved in a blur to stand in front of the heavy oak panel blocking the way.

"Cool your heels, lad." Munn tilted a hip and crossed arms over his chest. "The chief be occupied. Will summon you when ready to hear your report."

"But—"

"Whist! Chief in conference."

Damnation. The urge to kick something hard made everything within Gregor tense. Instead of lashing out, he sank against the cool stone of the wall and counted to ten, to one hundred. How long would the chief make him wait? He would have preferred to stay at Emily's bedside until she woke. Not for any other reason than to learn she was hale. *Oh, hell.* Who was he fooling? He wanted to gaze into those blue eyes again and see the lass smile. He wanted to kiss her lips. He wanted so much more than he ought.

Deep in the sensual imaginings wandering through his mind, he startled when a man—the castle priest—jostled past while departing from the chief's study.

"Gregor, did you hear me?" Archibald stood in the threshold sporting an impassive expression. "I am ready to receive your report."

Gregor pushed away from the wall and followed the chief into the chamber, where Duncan reclined in a chair before the hearth, whisky in hand. How much of the events of the day had the man already divulged to the chief? Had he recounted Gregor's encounters with fae magic? Would they send him back to Dunadd in disgrace?

"Sit. Make yourself comfortable." Archibald stepped to a table where a flagon and several cups sat. "Will you join us in a drink?"

"Nae. I thank you just the same, but I have duties to perform before I partake of the eve'n meal and find my pallet." Gregor chose to remain standing.

Archibald poured the amber liquid—*uisge-beatha*—into one of the cups and took a swallow. "Will be glad when this unpalatable day is at an end and I can take my rest in my lady-wife's embrace."

Gregor's cheeks heated, and he stared at the floor,

discomforted by the chief's candor.

"Dinnae fash yourself lad. You will understand when you take a wife."

"*Wife?*" Emily's image teased him. He inhaled a sharp breath and choked.

Both men stared at him with an uncomfortable intensity.

"Might be best if you sit." Archibald nodded to the chair opposite Duncan.

Gregor dropped to the cushioned seat, his gut twisting into a tight knot. This couldn't be good. "Perhaps a wee taste of the *water of life* will ease my throat."

Duncan guffawed.

Archibald cast a rigid glance at the big man. Duncan sobered and gave a slight nod in return. The chief handed Gregor a cup and raised his own. "Shall we drink to your upcoming nuptials?"

CHAPTER FOUR

*E*mily waded through the cobwebs of sleep, lingering in the fuzzy domain just beyond wakefulness. Something irritated her nose. She scrunched her nostrils trying to ease the prickle.

She sneezed. What on earth was that pungent herbal scent making her nose twitch? She opened her eyes expecting to be in her room at the inn with the window open to the garden.

The strong odor faded as an unfamiliar gray-haired woman stepped away from the bed. Emily wrinkled her brow. "Who are—"

"Em! You're awake." Tevin sat on the edge of the mattress beside her, eyes brimming with unshed tears. He lunged, hugging her tight, little fists clutching her sleeves.

"Oh, hi." Her voice sounded…feeble.

"I was so afraid you would never wake up."

A feminine chuckle made Emily jerk her gaze to… "Isobell? When did you arrive?"

"Tevin, I told you she would be fine." The ebony-haired beauty glided closer to the bed.

A velvet curtained, antique bed. Whose bed? Whose room? *Not mine. This is all wrong.*

"Tevin, give Emily some breathing space."

He slid to the side, gaze glued on her as if he feared she'd disappear before his eyes.

She sat bolt upright and slid back on the mattress, taking in the surroundings. Everything was strange. The furnishings antique yet new. None of the rooms at the inn had stone walls with slit wooden shutters covering the windows. And…this room had no lamps. Only candles lit the space, tainting the air with a burnt scent.

"Where am I?" She tried to sound nonchalant, but failed miserably.

"'Tis a long tale." Isobell dropped into a chair next to the bed. "Tevin, perhaps you would like to go play with Lach in the courtyard."

"Please let me stay with Em." He cuddled close to her side. He was definitely frightened of something, which made her nervous, too.

"What is going on, Isobell?" she asked. "Where are we?"

"You might want to brace yourself for what I have to tell you," Isobell said. "Please keep an open mind."

"You're scaring me."

"I dinnae mean to. It's just…" The woman hesitated as if gathering her thoughts. "You are at Castle Lachlan."

"That's impossible. Castle Lachlan is in Scotland. I haven't traveled to Scotland."

"We did, Em," Tevin blurted. "The little faeries brought us here."

"That's ridiculous. There are no such beings."

"The lad tells the truth, Emily. You have both travelled back through time to Scotland and the Year of our Lord 1521."

Emily frowned and shook her head. "It's not possible."

"'Tis. You must have heard rumors of strange happenings involving my in-laws, your employers, in Anderson Creek."

"Well, yeah, but I've never given the local gossip any credence."

"Perhaps you should." Isobell's husband Archie said as he strode into the room, looking so much like his twin brother Patrick from Anderson Creek, with his chestnut hair and muscular presence, Emily experienced a moment of confusion. Though rather than blue, this man's silver eyes gazed at her with compassion. "I am glad to see you are well, lass. This mornin' we feared for your health when you did not wake from your faint."

"I am fine. Thank you. But…"

The couple waited.

"Well, let me get this straight. You both expect me to believe faeries exist and have the ability to whisk people, against their will, through time and space on a whim?"

Isobell and Archie nodded, their features solemn.

"Told you so." Tevin crossed his arms over his chest and leaned back against the intricately carved headboard of the four poster bed, looking smug.

Had they all lost their minds?

"I have come to collect Tevin so Isobell can explain what we need of you, Emily," Archie said. "Come along, lad. Lach needs a sword sparring partner."

The boy hesitated, chewed on his bottom lip.

Emily ruffled his hair. "Go ahead, Tev. I'll be here when you are done. Just be careful. 'Kay?"

His frown burst into a grin. He nodded and joined Archie without a backward glance, bombarding the poor man with all sorts of questions.

She needed to get *her questions* answered. "So…"

"Do you remember anything from before you fainted?"

"It's a tad fuzzy." Emily massaged the ache building at her temples.

"You ken the mound behind the display garden at *Foxgloves*, aye? The one just beyond the garden gate?"

"Yeah. Iain warned me to never go there and to never allow the children to go there, but Tevin and Malcolm ran away from me during a heavy fog. I found them at the knoll and…"

"Then what?"

"Tevin vanished. I was standing there dumbfounded when Malcolm pushed me onto the mound and everything spun."

"That is the sensation of traveling through time. Although I understand everyone's experience is a wee different."

"How do you know all this?"

"Remember when Archie and I travelled to Anderson Creek years ago? Afterward, we returned here to your past. Our present."

"I can't even believe I'm in Scotland and you expect me to believe I traveled to the past?"

"Aye. Look out the window."

Emily cast aside a very real-feeling fur and slid from the bed. She walked across an authentic stone floor, threw open the shutters, and gasped. *Holy shit!* She leaned out over the stone sill. Sure enough she was in a castle that appeared to be surrounded by water. Across the waterway was a heather covered hill. Rustic cottages were grouped in a village of sorts. In the field below the window, men dressed in reenactment costumes slashed at each other with sharp-pointed swords—sun glinting on metal—like some of the men did in Anderson Creek.

An uber-attractive guy, with long brown hair of which many women would be envious, shot arrows at a muslin dummy, hitting the bulls-eye over the heart with each shot. Emily placed a hand on her stomach, feeling a tad queasy all of a sudden. He seemed so familiar.

"Are you feeling ill?" Isobell asked, voice laced with concern, as she came to stand behind Emily.

"Who is that guy with the bow?" *The one with the yummy, ass-hugging leather pants?*

The other woman chuckled softly. "That is Gregor, the lad who found you in the wood."

Emily spun around and faced her. "I admit this appears to be Scotland, but I don't remember traveling here. And, I certainly didn't travel through time."

"Come. Walk with me. I will give you a tour of the keep, and you will see I speak the truth."

Emily grasped Isobell's hand. "I don't mean to insult you."

"You have not. I felt as confused as you when I traveled through the faerie mound to the future." Isobell walked to the door and stopped. She glanced over a shoulder at Emily and frowned, turning back into the room. "This will not do. Your garments are all wrong." She opened a chest at the end of the bed and pulled out a linen gown. "Before you can be seen by the castle inhabitants, you must change into something more appropriate to this time. Archie believes the sheriff has placed a spy amongst us."

"Really, Isobell, aren't you taking this reenacting thing a bit far?"

"This is not make believe, Emily. You *are* in the past."

Emily glanced out the window again and chewed on her lip. "The men fighting in the yard do appear more...*fierce* than the reenactment guys in Anderson Creek."

"That is because they are more fearsome," Isobell said softly. "Their lives often depend on their skill with a weapon."

Emily accepted the garment and ran trembling fingers over the pale green fabric of a gown similar to the lavender dress Isobell wore, and akin to the dresses Elspeth sported at the living history exhibit during the Highland Games and Gathering of the Clans at Grandfather Mountain. Was Isobell telling the truth? With a heavy sigh, Emily removed her tunic-length hoodie, slipped the dress over her head and down her torso, covering her black lace trimmed bra, then shimmied out of the cotton leggings and slid the fine linen over her hips to drape just above the tops of her hiking boots.

"Did you bring anything modern with you besides your clothes? Perhaps a phone?"

"I dropped my cell when Malcom pushed me."

"Good. I guess no one will be aware of your modern undergarments." Isobell chuckled and helped with the lacings on the gown. "There. You look like a proper Highland lass."

"Now what?"

"I will show you the castle, and you will come to understand that you and Tevin are truly in Scotland, and in the past."

The circular stairs posed a challenge in the long gown. And the castle did appear to be lost in time. Still—

"Okay," Emily said. "I admit the rustic kitchen seems to imply the castle is not of our time, but—"

"Not of *your* time." Isobell guided her through the great hall. "It is exactly as it should be in *my* time. Castle Lachlan as you see it now is naught but a crumbling ruin in your time. That is why it is known in modern times as Old Castle Lachlan. This castle will fall into ruin after the MacLachlan chief is killed during the Battle of Culloden. Archie's descendants will build a new home on the mainland which will also be known as Castle Lachlan."

"How do you know such things?"

"Iain read to me from one of his many history books when I visited *your* future." Moisture pooled in Isobell's amethyst eyes, but the woman didn't shed a tear.

"I'm sorry. I didn't mean to make you sad. It must be terrible to know of awful things that will happen in the future."

Isobell's features brightened. "You finally believe?"

"Let's just say I'm begrudgingly considering the possibility that something otherworldly happened to me and Tevin." Emily tucked a stray hair behind an ear. "You mentioned a faerie mound."

"Aye. *Foxgloves'* garden gate and the mound beyond are enchanted by the Fae."

"Faeries really exist?"

"They do. As do other fae creatures such as—"

"Unicorns?"

"Perhaps. Though I dinnae really ken much about the horned beasts. I intended to tell you about Munn. Archie's wee man. He is a *brùnaidh*—a brownie. He found Tevin at the *Sithichean Sluaigh*, the faerie mound here in the Fir-wood, and brought the lad to us."

Before Emily could respond, Archie stepped from a doorway and signaled for them to join him.

Isobell touched Emily's sleeve. "Come. I believe Archie wants to introduce you to *your* savior."

CHAPTER FIVE

*E*mily stepped past Archie and entered the indicated room—a near medieval version of Patrick's study in Anderson Creek. A large parchment-strewn desk sat before a high window faced by two wooden chairs. A hearth—

A young man rose from one of the two chairs facing said hearth, and slowly turned toward her. She stumbled, almost losing her footing. *Oh my Lordy.* The long-haired guy she'd zeroed in on earlier from the bedroom window faced her. His intelligent gaze was piercing in its intensity.

He was even more breathtaking in person. Would his light brown hair feel silky to the touch? She flexed tingling fingers with the thought. She took a step toward him.

"Good day, mistress," he said.

Dear God! She melted on the spot, loving his yummy Scottish accent, getting lost in the dark pools that were his eyes. Eyes such a dark chocolate color they almost appeared black.

Isobell cleared her throat, bringing Emily back to her senses. Somewhat.

"U-um. Good day," Emily managed to sputter.

His full—very kissable—lips curved into a gorgeous smile. Her stomach did a slow jiggle.

"Glad I am to finally meet you properly," he said in that sinful deep voice. "I hope you can forgive me. I feared the worst after my—"

"'Twas hardly a proper introduction, lad." Archie laid a hand on his shoulder.

Emily frowned. There was something familiar about the long-haired guy. From before she'd seen him in the castle yard.

Ohmygod. In the woods. This is the guy who shot at me. With an arrow.

The certain memory surfaced in a rush. She jerked a hand to her ear. The fleshy edge stung like a minor burn. She stared at the clean fingers she withdrew, having half-expected them to be stained by blood.

"Let me make formal introductions," Archie continued, unaware of her mounting distress. "Emily, our lad here is Gregor. He—"

"You shot me with a *frigging* arrow," she sniped, ignoring Archie, her glare directed at the arrow-shooting idiot. Heat flushed her chest and face. She planted fisted hands on hips. "You could've killed me."

"I am truly sorry. 'Twas an accident, I assure you." He moved to step forward, but stopped as Archie held him in place.

"This is not a verra good start for a wedded union," the older man said.

"What?" She jerked her gaze to her host. "What union? What wedding?"

"Isobell, did you not inform Emily what is required of her?"

"I had nary a chance to explain the intrigues of this time before you summoned us to your side, husband."

Did they expect...

"Whoa. I'm not marrying anyone. Especially not him." Emily couldn't keep her lips from curling into a scowl. He'd shot at her as if she were a hunted animal, for God's sake. "You can send me and Tevin back to Anderson Creek.

Right?"

"'Tis not as easy as you might think." Isobell chewed on her bottom lip and exchanged a long glance with her husband. "The magic of the *Sithichean Sluaigh* only works on full moons—sometimes not even then—unless one of the Fae escorts a soul through."

"Which seems unlikely," Archie added. "Perhaps you should sit, lass, and hear what we have to say." He grasped her elbow and guided her to the chair next to the one the idiot who'd shot her had vacated. "Both of you should sit."

As she plopped onto the offered chair, the jerk dropped back into the seat to her right. His proximity was too close. The warmth of his presence pressed on her, making her jittery.

"I truly didn't mean to shoot at you," he said. "'Twas a pixie who interrupted my shot. Caused the arrow to release."

"Pixie? Are you for real?" He had to be nuts.

"Aye. A pixie." He held his hands about five inches apart. "A wee lass with wings."

"You expect me to believe a miniature woman with wings exists?"

"Several, to be sure," he added with a firm nod.

"And caused you to shoot me?" She tilted her head and frowned up at him.

His hair fell into his face with his vigorous nod, covering the ruddy color infusing his cheeks. She'd caught the deep blush before he turned away. She raised a hand to her mouth to hide an unexpected smile.

The guy was just so damn cute. Crazy. But cute.

Archibald dragged a chair over for Isobell, and the woman sat to Emily's left. "He speaks the truth," she said. "The wee creatures are known as the Pixie Clan."

Emily blinked. "You've seen them?"

"Nae." Isobell reached up and clasped her husband's hand, which rested on her shoulder.

The man sighed heavily. "You must understand, Emily, Scotland is rife with magic and those who wield its power. As your Tevin tells the tale, the pixies have taken an interest in you and the lad."

"He's a little boy. He makes up stories." She hastened a glance at the guy at her side. *Sometimes, so did big boys.*

"Not this time," Archie said.

Emily shook her head. "Even if I believed pixies existed—which I don't—why would they find me interesting enough to bother with? I lead a rather dull, quiet life in Anderson Creek. I spend my time working in the restaurant at the inn and taking care of the children. I ride my horse." *And mourn Kim's death.*

Archie ran a hand through his thick chestnut hair. "The pixies escorted you back in time for a purpose."

"Nefarious, I'm sure." She snorted. *Could she really believe any of this bullshit?*

"I wouldn't believe in them either if I had not seen them with my own eyes," Gregor said.

Emily jerked her gaze to the bow-wielding maniac. She needed to remember he'd shot at her. "Pixies?"

"Aye." He nodded. His honest gaze held hers. He believed he told the truth.

"Wow. You're blowing my mind." Emily massaged the ache building at her temples.

They each looked at her with furrowed brows as if she didn't make sense. Maybe she didn't. "I mean..." She swallowed uneasily, a whisper of acceptance taking hold. The evidence around her seemed to affirm she and Tevin were in the past and that some sort of *pixie magic* was the catalyst. "You've given me a lot to consider."

"There is more," Isobell said, her voice gentle as if cajoling a skittish colt. "You must wed Gregor. Sooner than later."

Emily's mouth fell open. Snapped shut. She glanced from face to face. "I'm sorry. I must have misheard. You don't really mean for me to marry a perfect stranger."

A grinding sound came from deep within Archie's throat. His firm gaze slid over her. "For your safety, you need to wed our lad here. Tales of magic shroud this clan. The Sheriff of Bute has embarked on a crusade against Clan MacLachlan and watches for new rumors to surface. He would be more than happy to accuse you of delving into the dark arts."

"Witchcraft?"

"Aye. Although many folk fear the magic surrounding us, the sheriff's motives are purely political. He will use any whispering of odd occurrences against us. Against you. But if you are wed to a Highlander… Ach, well, you and Tevin will be safer with Gregor claiming you as wife and Tevin as son."

"And you have agreed?" She pinned Gregor with a surprised stare. The guy could probably have any woman he wanted. *Why would he want me?*

He held a closed fist over his heart. "I would be honored to be your champion."

His declaration was rather sweet. Heroic. But still…

"How will being married to…" She gulped. "Gregor. How will being *married* protect us?"

"We need you to blend in. Not attract attention," Archie said. "You ken a beautiful maiden such as yourself will stir interest amongst the single lads. Your modern ways are different. Fascinating. Enticing. The lads will compete for your favor. Rumors will circulate and reach the sheriff's ears. He is far too interested in the comings and goings of our keep. He accused Jillian of witchcraft and arrested her when she visited several years ago. She managed to escape with Stephen's help and that of the Fae. But it was a near thing."

Emily shook her head, overwhelmed by the insane circumstances. "Fae? Pixies? Witchcraft? This is madness."

Archie leaned forward. "I dinnae ken if I can protect you if the sheriff decides—"

"Please, lass," Gregor implored. "Let me help you and the wee lad."

"I can't marry you. I can't marry anyone." She couldn't betray Kim's memory with another man. Especially one as handsome as Gregor. She snapped her gaze to Archie. "I won't."

Emily ran from the room.

"Wait!" Gregor's voice trailed her.

She hoped they—*he*—wouldn't follow. Could she be any more upset? More embarrassed? They had planned to force the guy to marry her. It wasn't as if he was attracted to her. They'd just met. She skidded across the great hall's stone floor and rushed down a flight of stairs and out of the keep chased by overwhelming panic. How was she to get out of this insane nightmare?

CHAPTER SIX

*T*he meeting with his intended hadn't gone well. Gregor swirled the amber liquid in the glass the chief had given him earlier, trying to appear unaffected by the lass's rejection. Then he threw back a long swallow of the whisky, taking solace from the slow burn in his throat.

Lady Isobell frantically whispered in the chief's ear. She turned to Gregor. "I will speak to her." The lady rushed from the chamber in pursuit of Emily.

Gregor rose to his full five foot ten inch height to follow, surprised at how much he wanted the lass to agree to become his wife. He didn't mind that the chief hadn't given him a chance to refuse. That Gregor hadn't intended to wed until after he'd made a name for himself within the clan. The order had been given and he had accepted without complaint. He'd been mesmerized by the lass since first glimpsing her on that cursed knoll.

"Dinnae chase after her," Archibald advised. "Give her time."

"Do we have time?"

"Nae." The chief shook his head. "Not much anyway."

Gregor stalked to the window and ran the tips of his fingers over his forehead and scalp, digging in with blunt

38

nails, massaging, and tugging the strands of long hair back from his eyes. The sun shone brightly from a cloudless blue sky. On the field below, the MacLachlan lads practiced with all manner of weapons, the day proceeding in a normal, orderly manner as was usual during the month of August.

However, naught would ever be the same for him or for the lass. The sooner she accepted the truth of their situation, the better he could provide protection.

Emily stumbled across the cobbled courtyard and through the castle gate into a field of men brandishing lethal-looking swords and other weapons not of the twenty-first century. She froze. These men were definitely not reenactors. These men were real honest-to-goodness Scottish warriors.

Holy shit!

One bare-chested man brushed past, his plaid riding up a muscled thigh as he attacked another scarcely clad man, their swords connecting with a clang. Her startled yelp went unheeded, as did the flush heating her cheeks. The men bounded away without acknowledging her presence.

As if she needed more proof she was out of her element; in a time not her own.

Emily backed into the modest safety of the gateway and lifted a hand to her brow to cut the glare from the sun. Where was Tevin?

Ah. There he is.

On the opposite side of the field, he and another boy—likely Archie and Isobell's son—pranced about in the same manner as the men, only the boys lunged at each other with dull wooden swords. Circling and thrusting. Then repeating the moves. Moves Tevin probably learned from his father or some of the other Scottish reenactors in Anderson Creek.

A gnarled man of dwarf stature, with dark skin and dressed in the greens and browns of the forest, watched their practice from a perch on a nearby stone wall, his weathered face drawn in a tight frown. She wondered who he was and why he appeared so cross.

Emily lost sight of the children when several men broke away from their individual fights and encircled the boys, cheering them on. Bellowing, hooting, and howling.

She set off across the field, the need to hurry to Tevin's side tightening her chest, but the annoying long skirt of her gown wrapped around and tangled between her legs, slowing her progress. Kicking at the fabric, Emily growled—gathered the cloth in a fisted hand, tugged it to one side and up to thigh height, freeing her legs—and ran. When she reached the boisterous crowd, she bobbed to the left and right, trying to see through the wall of sweaty and stinky bodies surrounding the boys.

She finally found a spot where she could see over a shorter man's shoulder by way of standing on tiptoe. Only to see the blunt tip of his opponent's sword poke Tevin in the chest, and Tevin fall to the ground arms spread wide. Eyes fluttering shut.

"No!" Emily's heart plunged into her belly and she rushed forward. *Dear God.* Was he badly hurt? She pushed and shoved at the men blocking the way. It was like trying to burst through an impenetrable wall. *Dammit!* She needed to get to Tevin.

The crowd of men merged into a tight group and lifted the winner onto their shoulders. She was pushed back and nearly knocked to the ground as they carried the boy away, tramping about the field in a victory march, shouting in Gaelic, a language she didn't understand. If she'd known she would unwittingly travel back in time to the Highlands of Scotland, she would have asked one of those in Anderson Creek fluent in the language to teach it to her.

She stumbled. By the time she caught her balance and made her way the short distance to Tevin, a blond-haired man had offered a hand to the boy. Tevin jumped to his feet with exuberance, an impish grin breaking across his face. The two shared a few quiet words, then the man strutted away.

Emily must have blinked, for the next thing she knew the

very small man who a moment before had sat on the wall now stood in front of Tevin, hands fisted on leather clad hips, an ugly glower adding wrinkles upon wrinkles to his face. "Keep your distance from Ciaran," he ordered. "He does not have the chief's favor."

"But he said he would take me to Ben Nevis," Tevin whined.

"'Tis a long way from here and nae place for a wee *bairn* like you. 'Tis dangerous."

"I'm not a baby," Tevin grumbled. "He said it's where the orange dragon has its lair. That its horde is full of gold and jewels."

"I told you." The man wagged a finger at Tevin. "And the chief told you. Dragons dinnae exist. Ciaran naught but teased you."

"But—"

"Whist! Nae more talk of dragons."

Tevin's shoulders drooped.

Emily bit back a smile, not wanting to bruise the boy's feelings. "Are you hurt?" She crouched to his height and gently grasped his upper arms to hold him in place. "You nearly scared me to death when you fell."

"I fell on purpose."

"Why on earth did you do that?"

"Wouldn't be right to best the chief's son and win," Tevin said with a smirk.

"Humpf!" The little man crossed his arms over his chest.

Emily ruffled Tevin's hair. Mud caked his chest and his kilt. "Ugh. You smell like the men and like you've been hanging in the stables."

He shrugged, showing no remorse.

"Now listen," she said. "No more talk about hunting dragons. They don't exist. Okay?"

His smile vanished and he stared at the ground, dragging a foot back and forth across the loose dirt. He mumbled something she didn't catch.

"Tevin?"

"All right." He pursed his lips.

"And if this man here—"

"His name is Munn. And he's a brownie," Tevin said as if she should have known as much.

Perhaps she should have known considering the man had pointed ears like an elf, and wore pointy green boots on oversized feet and a pointed green cap on his head. He reminded her of a court jester she'd seen in one of those popular historical period series DVDs she borrowed from the library.

"Well, if Munn says you should stay away from that Ciaran guy, then you should stay away from him."

The brownie gave a quick nod. Twirled in a circle and…disappeared.

What the hell? Emily blinked. Shook her head. "Did *he* just vanish into thin air?"

"Yep. He does that. He's a brownie."

"So you said." She shuddered. "We need to go home. Can you remember how to get back to the mound where we arrived?"

"I think so."

"Good. Where's your shirt?"

"It was too hot to wear it to fight." He dashed to the foot of the wall and grabbed the polo and his dirty sweatshirt from the ground.

She followed and helped him pull both over his head. "Let's hurry back to the mound and go home. 'Kay?"

"That wouldn't be wise," Isobell said.

Emily spun about. She hadn't heard the woman approach. Would Isobell try to stop them from leaving?

CHAPTER SEVEN

*B*ack in the bedroom assigned to her, Emily massaged the tense fingers of one hand with those of the other while waiting for a maid to prepare a bath. Isobell had impressed upon her the risk of running off half-cocked alone through unknown terrain with a child who couldn't possibly remember the way to the faerie knoll. Since no one at the castle would defy an order from their chief and oblige her and Tevin with escort to the mound, Emily had agreed under duress to accept the hospitality of Castle Lachlan for another night's stay.

"Please," Isobell said. "Reconsider Gregor's offer to take you as wife."

Emily frowned and shook her head. Why didn't they understand?

"Do you have an intended in your future time?" the other woman pressed.

"Not exactly. I planned to marry Kim in the fall. You might remember him from the inn. He bartended in the lounge. Anyway…" Emily's voice quivered. "He was diagnosed with brain cancer several months ago, and died."

Just mentioning *it* made her chest constrict with remembered pain.

"I am sorry for your loss, but that leaves you with little reason to reject Gregor's proposal. Jillian and Stephen, as well as the others, are likely frantic about you and Tevin's disappearance, however, they are well aware of the fickle nature of the Fae and of the *Sithichean Sluaigh*. They each had similar ordeals years ago. They would wish us and *you* to do whatever possible to ensure yours and Tevin's safety. A marriage with Gregor would help."

Emily had no response. There had to be another way.

Isobell's heavy sigh ratcheted up the guilt niggling at Emily.

Even if she could forgive him for shooting at her with an arrow—which she couldn't—she didn't *want* to marry Gregor. It wouldn't matter if he was the best catch in all of Scotland circa 1521. She didn't want to marry anyone. Especially someone she'd only recently met. She couldn't disrespect Kim's memory. She still loved him. His sudden illness and as sudden death had left a hole in her chest and her heart broken in a zillion tiny pieces. She couldn't marry someone else. Even if it was only in name.

Besides she wasn't staying in this time. She and Tevin were going home.

No. They couldn't make her do something she didn't want to do.

"Your bath is ready, mistress."

Emily gave the maid a tenuous smile. "Thank you."

"I will take Tevin to Lach's chamber," Isobell said. "See he is cleaned up and fed. He can stay there for the night, allowing you some privacy."

"Would you like that, Tev?" Emily bit her lip, worried about the child. Though he seemed to be enjoying the adventure.

"Sure." His eyes lit, and he nodded with enthusiasm.

"Okay. Off with you then," Emily said. "I'll see you later, Isobell?"

"Aye. I will return to assist you in dressing for the eve'n meal." Isobell ushered a yawning Tevin from the room.

The maid helped Emily undress and climb into the tub. The inviting water was a perfect temperature and, with herbs floating on the surface, smelled like the summer gardens at *Foxgloves*, the garden center at home in Anderson Creek. How she missed home.

She dismissed the wistful thought and concentrated on the here and now. She sank into the soothing water and sighed. The soap the maid handed her gave off a pleasant lavender scent and was gentler to the skin than Emily would have imagined.

"I will wash your hair if you are ready," the maid said after a short time.

Enjoying the pampering, Emily agreed. "Thank you."

The young woman gathered the damp strands to the back of Emily's head and used a dipper ladle to wet the mass from a bucket. "Yer hair is such a rich brown color, and so verra fine to the touch. Yer new husband will be well pleased."

Emily stiffened. "I'm not getting married."

Why were they all pushing so hard for her to marry? What was in it for them?

"Please forgive me. I did not mean to overstep. I had heard ye were to wed the braw Gregor on the morrow. I suppose 'twas naught but idle gossip amongst the kitchen lasses."

Emily certainly hoped that was the case. "I have not consented to a marriage."

"'Tis a shame. There are many who would wish to be in yer place."

Let them have him.

Why didn't that thought sit well? Why did it make her stomach clench? Emily pursed her lips, annoyed with her contrary feelings.

The maid lathered soap in Emily's hair, massaged the scalp, and poured a bucket of warm water over her head to rinse away the suds. "I should collect more drying cloths," the maid said when finished. "Can you manage on yer own for a wee while?"

"I'll be fine. Go ahead. I'll soak for a bit and relax." *And forget about all this talk of marriage. Forget about the handsome Gregor.*

"Verra good." The maid left the heavy oak door cracked.

The draw from the opening dragged a warm summer breeze from the gaping window. The draft raised gooseflesh on Emily's exposed skin, making her shiver although she wasn't cold. She leaned back against the rim of the tub and let the warm water sooth stiff muscles. Her mind whirred. How was she to get out of this mess?

After a while, she became weightless as if she were about to doze off.

Tee teehee hee. Tee teehee hee. Tee teehee hee.

A soft buzzing and a tinkling giggle jerked her eyes wide open. Her pulse raced. "Who's there?"

A dragonfly hovered in front of her face.

No. No way! The bug couldn't—but it did. The diminutive creature had a beautiful, tiny human face and tiny human hands and tiny human feet. Gossamer lavender wings edged with deep purple kept her aloft.

Tee teehee hee.

The pixie blew dust into Emily's face, causing her to gasp and suck the particles deep into her lungs. She choked and coughed. The tiny creature darted away in a frantic flutter of wings and flew out the window, leaving behind a befogged Emily with only one thought on her mind as she eased back against the rim of the tub—Gregor.

Gregor strode through the passageway surprised when he reached his destination to find the bedchamber door assigned to Emily ajar. He knocked on the wood, and the oak panel creaked farther open, exposing to view the most delightful sight.

Emily's blue eyes—eyes that haunted him since the first— fluttered open.

She smiled. "Oh, hi."

Gregor was taken aback by the pleasant greeting.

The lass seemed different. Her gaze held a tenderness that hadn't been there earlier. As if she was glad to see him. His mouth went dry, and he had to clear a parched throat. He hesitated, trying to remember why he had sought her out.

"I probably shouldn't be here, but…" He raked a hand through his tangled hair. Did he really believe interrupting her bath would help plead his case? "I thought we could talk and perhaps I might convince you to accept an apology for my misplaced shot."

"Forgiven and forgotten," she said, still smiling.

"That is good. Thank you." He exhaled a short breath. "As to my offer of marriage. I wish you would reconsider my heartfelt proposal. I wish only to ensure your safety and that of the *bairn*."

Not true. He desired much more.

He swallowed uneasily. He shouldn't be staring at her as if he was a green lad again and found himself in the company of the most comely lass at the fair. He definitely shouldn't be gazing upon her while she bathed. An immediate arousal had him shifting his weight. Thank the Saints above, he no longer wore his leather *trews* and had donned a *plaide*. The lass would remain unaware of his ardor.

"You are kind," she said.

"I should not be here. I had not realized you bathed." He stumbled over the words. "Should leave."

"No. Come in." A dainty hand waved him forward.

Unable to deny her, he stepped through the threshold. Awkward. Unsure how to proceed.

"Will you close the door?" she asked. "When open, it causes a draft from the window."

He hesitated. Many would believe it wrong for him to be alone with her with the door shut. Especially with her state of undress. She would be compromised. He didn't mind as long as she seemed unconcerned. He'd be the one to benefit if the chief forced her hand.

Gregor had always thought it unfair an unwed lass could

attend to the bath of a man, but the same woman was forbidden to be attended by a man. He closed the door, took a deep breath, and turned toward the lass he yearned to take as wife. Once wed, they could attend to each other's bathing without censure.

The intimate thought brought warmth to his chest and fire to his blood.

"Come closer," she said. "We're to be married after all."

His eyes widened. Had he heard correctly? He forced the shock from his features and glanced at Emily from under lowered lashes. Had she noted his reaction?

"Have you changed your mind then?" he managed to ask in a steady voice, concealing a fervor of hope.

Sometimes he found her words confusing, but he felt certain she'd claimed they were to wed. He took several steps deeper into the chamber. Inhaled sharply. Froze. Stared into the tub. Although the herbs floating on the surface shadowed her breasts, the moist skin above—caressed by lapping water when she moved—was most appealing.

"Had I misunderstood?" Her brow furrowed. "I thought we had agreed to marry tomorrow."

He jerked his intent gaze from the moisture shimmering on her skin to her bemused eyes.

When had she changed her mind? Why hadn't he been told?

He cleared his throat. Moistened his lips. "Aye. We are in agreement. We wed on the morrow in the chapel directly after breaking our fast at a wedding feast."

"Gregor, what are you doing in here?" Lady Isobell said as she strode into the chamber, carrying a stack of drying cloths. "You ken 'tis not fitting for you to be alone with Emily while she bathes, and especially with the door closed."

Although Lady Isobell quoted the tenets of proper behavior, her tone contained only token censure. The edges of her lips quivered as if she struggled to suppress a smile.

"You will be pleased to learn Emily has agreed to become my wife." He shot a grin her direction then glanced back at the beautiful woman who'd just made him the happiest man at Castle Lachlan. "Perhaps, Mistress Emily, you would walk with me at sunrise and allow me to show you the walled garden before we break our fast and wed?"

"I'm sure to enjoy that." She beamed.

He rubbed his chest. Her easy agreement made him feel strange. *Good.*

"Excellent. I have missives to send." He bowed and bounded from the chamber, a bounce to his step.

CHAPTER EIGHT

*O*nly the slightest of morning light stole through the window of Emily's room when Isobell and two other woman arrived full of excitement to prepare her for the wedding. Emily yawned. Why hadn't Gregor joined them last night for dinner?

She turned from the window and the niggling thought to the three expectant faces. Isobell held the gown Emily was to wear. "It's a lovely dress. Thank you for lending it to me."

"The color goes well with your blue eyes. The gown was made for Elspeth." Isobell ran slim fingers over the lustrous silk fabric. "Many years ago, Archie brought several bolts of fine cloth back from France for his sister. He had been on embassage for the king with the Campbells, and Elspeth had been betrothed to the Campbell's second son. Of course, that was before we were wed, and before Elspeth refused to abide by the old contract and handfasted with Finn." She leaned toward Emily and whispered near her ear. "That was before they traveled to the future."

The pale dress reminded Emily of a moonstone brooch often worn by Elspeth in Anderson Creek. It was a shame no one from home would see Emily wearing the gown. If only she hadn't lost her cell phone before falling through time.

Tevin could have taken a picture for them to share on their return.

She wrinkled her brow. Why was she getting married if they were going home?

Could Gregor travel back with them?

"I am delighted you have reconsidered your position and agreed to wed with Gregor," the other woman said, startling her from the disturbing questions rattling around in her brain. "He is a braw lad. He will keep you and Tevin safe."

Emily rubbed her forehead where a nagging ache pulsed over her eyes. Her mind went fuzzy. What had she been thinking?

"I'm sorry. What did you say?" she asked.

"'Tis not important. 'Twas a surprise you decided to wed with Gregor after fervently denying the possibility."

Why did Isobell and Gregor act as if she changed her mind? She'd agreed from the beginning it would be for the best. Who wouldn't want to marry a man as gorgeous as Gregor? Or as nice?

"I'm sure he will guard us well."

She hoped he'd perform other husbandly duties well, too.

Would they make love tonight? The thought made her insides tighten with anticipation.

Isobell dropped the dress over Emily's head and shoulders. Fortunately, the women couldn't see the scarlet color that must be blushing her cheeks from her risqué imaginings. The silk slipped smoothly over her hips and draped to the floor, the sensuous touch of the fabric against bare skin making her feel beautiful.

"I am a bit uneasy having pressured you." Isobell stepped away. Her critical gaze slid over Emily from head to bare foot. She nodded with approval, a genuine smile curving her lips. "You see, I refused to wed with Archie on the eve of our marriage."

"Really? Why?"

"I was angry. Proud. I didn't want to be told what to do by a man I nae longer trusted, one who nae longer trusted me. He ordered me put in the dungeon until I reconsidered my position and agreed to wed him."

"He didn't? That's horrible."

"Not so bad. Really. Munn came to me, offering a fine wine. 'Twas the best wine I had ever tasted. 'Twas spelled by magic. You ken? Made me verra agreeable."

"So then what happened?"

"We wed. But when the wine wore off, I was verra, verra angry with Archie and ran away. I was a foolish lass. 'Twas a snowy night. A dangerous night to be abroad. I became entranced by a strange light, which guided me through the blustery snow to the *Sithichean Sluaigh*, the knoll of the Fae. On the knoll, 'twas like spring, and I stumbled through time to Anderson Creek." She waved a hand in dismissal. "All of that has long been forgotten and I love my husband and *bairns* verra much. Shall we do your hair?"

"Yes. But tell me how you and Archie got back together."

"He came after me. He always will. As will *your* Gregor."

"He's not mine. He only agreed to marry me because Archie forced him. He doesn't have real feelings for me. He couldn't. We just met."

"And you? Do you have *real* feelings for him?"

Did she? Maybe. "Like I said, we just met."

"Good marriages have been based on less."

The older of the women held a length of plaited yellow flowers and ribbons to be woven through Emily's hair while the other worked to entwine the garland through looped braids pinned atop her head. The pineapple-like fragrance tickled her nose.

After the women were satisfied with her appearance, Emily followed Isobell down the circular stairs, careful of her footing. The long gown made the descent in skimpy slippers risky. She huffed a breath when they reached the lower floor. At the entrance to the great hall, she stopped, searching for Gregor's form among those men already gathered, her emotions all aflutter.

There he is.

The hairs on the back of Gregor's neck stood on end with awareness. *Emily.* He spun around, and there she stood just within the doorway, stealing his breath with her beauty.

He strode toward her with purpose. Grasping her small hand within his much larger, calloused one, he bowed, breathing a light kiss on the tips of her fingers.

A lovely blush brightened her cheeks.

"Shall we?" He crooked an arm, offering escort.

She gave a quick nod and rested her fingers on his forearm with the lightest of touches, allowing his guidance down a short flight of stairs and into the gloom of the courtyard shaded by stark castle walls. They slipped through the gate and into the yard and were greeted by the golden rays of the rising sun.

He blinked. Emily shaded her eyes with her free hand.

Several *currachs* carried a party of men across the small bay, lads straining at the oars as they cut through an unusually rough surf to beach on the opposite shore.

An angry sound growled from his throat before he could stop the sour utterance.

Emily stiffened. "What is wrong?"

"Naught. I am sorry." He used his free hand to pat the fingers resting on his arm. "I am glad to see Ciaran leave. 'Tis all."

"You sounded more angry than glad."

"The man has a penchant for irritating folks."

"Ciaran? That name seems familiar."

"Aye. He has been filling Lach and Tevin's heads with fantasies this past day about treasure and dragons in the mountains northeast of here."

"Oh no. Tevin believes his destiny is to kill an orange dragon."

"Ach, well, we are free of Ciaran for a while. His duty takes him far from Castle Lachlan."

"That is probably for the best." Emily relaxed. "What are those unusual boats in which the men travel?"

"They are *currachs* made of wicker and skins. Those at the castle often use the wee crafts to travel back and forth to the mainland. 'Tis how I brought you here."

"I'm sorry. My manners have been lacking. Thank you for rescuing me."

"'Twas my pleasure, mistress."

"We'll be married in a few hours. Shouldn't you address me just as Emily?"

"If that is your wish." Warmth infused his chest.

"It is."

"Perhaps after we swear our vows before the priest we will cross to the stables and ride to a hunting lodge tucked in the Fir-wood not far from here. The chief has given me leave to spend several days alone with you to celebrate our nuptials. Would you enjoy such a jaunt?" The thought of what they would do while at the lodge made his blood thicken. He hoped she was amenable.

Emily jounced on her heels, pulled her hand away, and hugged him quick.

Mercy. He tightened a slackened jaw. He liked this exuberant Emily very much indeed.

"Oh! Thank you." She once again placed her hand sedately on his arm. "That would be wonderful. I miss my horse."

He guided her along the path toward the garden. Did only the chance to ride interest her? "You have your own horse in the land you come from?"

"Yes. You sound surprised. His name is Black Pepper."

Piobar Dubh. "Your family must be wealthy."

She shrugged. "Middle class, but I received a small inheritance from my grandmother, which pays for his upkeep."

Gregor had no idea what middle class meant, and he worried, mayhap, they didn't suit. He still didn't quite understand all the chief tried to explain about her circumstances. Would she be happier with someone from her own land?

They continued along the path in silence, his previous eagerness subdued.

Did he really want to wed a stranger? From a faraway land? And if he understand correctly, from another time? Though he could barely credit such a fanciful notion.

At the garden archway, he slipped her hand into his and entered first to ensure naught was awry. He'd vowed to keep her safe.

"Oh, this is lovely," she said as they traversed the path through the garden beds filled with vegetables and herbs to the rose garden, where he seated her on the turf bench, abloom with small, fragrant white flowers. The gentle scent was heady. As was her beauty.

"I owe you an apology," she said.

He frowned. "Whatever for?"

"For not believing your story about the pixies."

"I guess 'tis hard to believe in something you have never seen."

"I saw one last night."

Her admission made his brows rise. "You did?"

"Yeah. In my room, while I was bathing. Before you came. She wore a purple gown and had sheer lavender wings. Like that one there." Emily pointed to a dragonfly-like creature perched on a shiny rose leaf.

He held out a hand and the ebony-haired pixie jounced onto his palm.

Tee teehee hee. Tee teehee hee. Tee teehee hee.

The wee creature's voice tinkled like the sweetest chimes.

"Here is another!" Emily leapt to her feet and held out a hand. A blonde pixie with green wings landed on an outstretched finger. "This one has iridescent peridot wings."

Gregor brought his hand closer to his face for a better look at the one he held.

Emily did the same with hers. "Hello," she murmured.

Tee teehee hee. The pixies giggled again, before blowing dust into their faces. Then with more giggles, they flew away, high over the garden wall.

Emily and Gregor sneezed in unison, and then dropped onto the bench, overcome with laughter. Tears of merriment streamed from both their eyes.

"They are so cute," Emily said, when she sobered.

"The gemstone in your wedding ring is the same color as the green pixie's wings. I sent a missive to my father last night requesting it be brought here in all due haste. I fear I must present you with a temporary, lesser quality substitute at the ceremony today. I doubt my mother's gold ring will arrive in time."

"A peridot. How lovely." Emily twisted on the seat to look directly at him. "Your mother's ring?"

"She passed many years ago during childbirth."

"I'm sorry." Compassion filled her gaze. "Your father? Should the wedding be postponed until he arrives? I don't know much about you and nothing about your family. Don't you think that odd?"

"I dinnae ken much about you or your family either. We will each learn about the other as time allows." He flexed his shoulders. "The chief would not want the wedding postponed. And it is likely the ring will be sent with a messenger. My father is Allain of Dunadd. He is kept busy overseeing Dunadd, another of the Clan MacLachlan holdings."

A loud horn blast sounded, and Emily startled.

"They summon us to our wedding meal." Gregor stood and held out a firm hand to Emily. They were about to embark on a new chapter in their lives.

CHAPTER NINE

*M*unn waited. Even though he remained invisible, he hid behind a leafy bush until Gregor and the lass from the future passed and made their way along the footpath to the castle.

Confident with the knowledge they couldn't see him, he hurried through the archway and into the walled garden, emerging into his physical form. His nose twitched as he sniffed the air, drawing in the varied odors. He traversed the main garden path, passing vegetable and herb beds. His leg brushed a thyme plant, and its tangy scent reached his nostrils. Extending an arm downward, he broke off a sprig and stuffed it inside the sleeve of his *leine*.

He passed the garden's well and a bed of declining strawberry plants. With a deep inhale, he tested the air again. The closer he got to the rose garden, the stronger the treacly scent of faerie dust—a sweeter fragrance than that of the white chamomile flowers covering the turf bench. Too sweet for his liking.

He stood within the semi-circle of thorny bushes hands fisted on hips. What enchantment had been evoked this day by Mercail and her pesky pixies' potent powder?

The serving folk in the castle whispered, spreading the rumor that Gregor would wed the lass from the future after the morning meal. Nuptials *encouraged* by the chief, they claimed. Had pixie dust made the couple agreeable?

Had Oonagh, the Queen of the Fae, drawn Marcail into her manipulative schemes and set her up as matchmaker since Caitrina was no longer beholden to the queen?

Doubtful. Oonagh would never stoop so low as to entrust her machinations to the impetuous wee folk. She'd more than likely entice one of the lesser faeries to do her bidding.

Arms crossed, Munn paced the length of the turf bench and back. Then, again. What was he to do?

If Marcail and her clan had gone rogue, Oonagh's fury would be epic.

And on whom would she take out her wrath?

Munn. That's who.

His duty was to protect Clan MacLachlan, but how could he stop the wedding without angering the chief? He'd tried on other occasions to stop MacLachlan men from marrying the wrong women and failed. And where had that gotten him? *Nowhere.*

Nowhere, but into a tub of trouble with the queen.

He huffed out a long breath and glanced at the sky. Dark clouds blew in from the east, chasing away the warmth of the sun. A portent of events to come?

Caitrina would ken what to do about the pixies. She was needed here in Scotland. *Now.*

Munn removed the thyme sprig from his sleeve, tore off a few fragrant leaves, and chewed on them to release their essential oil. He savored the agreeably pungent flavor on his tongue. The task he would undertake this day required courage.

He spun in a circle, sucking decaying garden debris into the whirlwind surrounding him, and then vanished from mortal sight, becoming mere particles traveling on the wind. Arriving in the Fir-wood, he stumbled head over foot then crashed to the ground where he tumbled several times across the grassy mound of the *Sithichean Sluaigh* before coming to a stop and landing on his rump with a, "*Humph!*"

An aggressive shake of the head cleared blurred vision. He flicked his gaze about the mound, swiveling his head this way and that. No footprints marred the perfection of the grassy hill. Munn inhaled a deep breath, deciphering traces of lingering scents. Duncan. Gregor. The lass from the future. The musk of a stag. Fae magic vibrated in the air, but nary a sign that Caitrina had visited the knoll during these past several years.

Damn that infuriating faerie. Where was the halfling princess when needed?

He pushed to his feet and marched to the center of the knoll, inhaled a deep breath, and concentrated. Pressure built. Pain pounded within his skull. He thrust his remaining energy into crafting a message, and sent it across realms.

A high-pitched wailing assaulted his ears. Agony unimaginable. He clamped clammy hands to the sides of his head. An anguished moan escaped his suddenly parched lips. A tingly numbness invaded his limbs. His legs faltered and he crumbled to the ground in a lifeless heap.

Moments passed. Minutes. Finally, he found the strength to rise to a sitting position and open his eyes. Wisps of pastel color hovered in the air—yellows, pinks, blues.

Summons sent. But had it been received?

CHAPTER TEN

Castle Lachlan

*P*alms moist, Emily waited with Isobell in the passageway outside the MacLachlan family chapel. Breakfast in the great hall had passed in a happy blur. Afterward, she joined Gregor, along with Archie, Isobell, and the clan priest, in the chief's study to sign marriage documents. Her stomach raged with turmoil and she thought to bolt, but when the time came for her signature, she took the quill from Gregor's steady hand with only a moment's hesitation.

Having put ink to parchment made everything seem so very real. A shiver skittered over Emily's tense shoulders. Was she *really* about to marry Gregor?

"Are you chilly, my dear?" Isobell asked "Would you like me to fetch a wrap?"

"I'm fine." Emily shot her hostess a quick smile. A smile she didn't feel.

It wasn't too late. If she left before they said their vows—

Her head throbbed. She rubbed her temples, trying to remember what she'd been thinking. Movement caught her attention.

Munn skulked along the hallway toward them, mumbling

under his breath. When he noticed them standing there, he jerked to a halt, his lips thinned and his forehead wrinkled into thick creases, as though her presence caused him great consternation. He made an abrupt turnabout and disappeared in a blur of brown and green fabric.

Emily shook her head. Such a strange little man.

She peered into the empty chapel. Even at this mid-morning hour, candles lit the room. A door to the side of the cloth-covered altar opened. The priest entered, knelt before the altar, made the sign of the cross, stood, and faced the same door of which he had entered. The door was a private entry to the chapel from the chief's study where the men had remained after the signing to discuss pressing clan business while she and Isobell had withdrawn to the passageway to wait. Gregor appeared in the doorway next. Followed by Archie and Tevin. All three dressed in light colored tunics and draped in plaid cloth of the same blue, red, and black. Golden light from the candles flickered and flashed, causing their shadows to dance upon gilded walls and furnishings.

Emily's insides quivered. She wet her lips. Pinched her cheeks. *She could do this. She could.*

Gregor's dark gaze circled the room, landing on her. His pleased smile helped quell the riot of nerves bent on keeping her immobile.

The light pressure from Isobell's palm against the small of her back encouraged her to proceed. Emily swallowed, summoned inner strength, and stepped across the threshold.

Her husband-to-be strode forward and grasped her hand. "Your beauty leaves me breathless."

A thrilled gasp of surprise escaped her lips. The smile she leveled on him came from the heart. "You are quite handsome yourself this morning."

His grin took her breath away. Made her realize there was nowhere else she'd rather be this morning than here with Gregor.

"Thank you for agreeing to become my wife." He gently squeezed her hand, bowed, and brushed a kiss across the tips of her fingers.

An electric tingle hummed up her arm. Lit up her nervous system. Made her heart lurch.

His eyes widened. He must have felt a similar sensation.

What should she say?

He obviously didn't expect a reply for he guided her toward the altar.

The priest greeted them with a nod then looked beyond them to the few who came to witness their union. "Are there any among you with reason this couple should not wed?"

There was a shuffle of feet behind them and a soft cough, but no one spoke up against their marriage. Emily released the breath she held.

"Please kneel." The priest indicated two embroidered velvet pillows that had been placed on the stone floor before the altar.

Gregor assisted her to her knees. He knelt beside her, keeping possession of her hand and interlacing their fingers. His warmth soothed the flutter in her stomach.

The priest turned to the altar and held up a narrow, hemmed length of cloth made from the same plaid the men wore. He bowed in prayer then turned back to them and tied the cloth around the wrists of their entwined hands. "This cloth binds your love together."

Emily flicked a glance at Gregor. He gave a quick nod, and she returned attention to the priest. The priest's words seeded hope in her heart. She and Gregor would find love together. Perhaps he was the reason the pixies brought her to the past.

The service flashed by in an instant. It was time for the reciting of vows.

The priest bade them to stand and removed the fabric that had bound them together. She knew what was coming next. She hated that she didn't have a ring for Gregor. He assisted her to her feet and remained facing her, the silver ring he held glittered in the candlelight. His gaze softened. "With this ring—"

The crash from the back of the chapel, as the heavy door slammed against the stone wall, made Emily jump and swing around to see what caused the commotion.

"One moment, please." A handsome fiftyish man with graying hair covered with the dust of travel strode into the chapel. With an abrupt nod to the priest, he genuflected before the altar, then dragged Gregor into a bear of a hug. After several backslaps on both sides, the man bowed to Emily. "Mistress."

With a wrinkled brow, she watched him step away into the small group at the back of the chapel. Who on earth?

"Emily." Gregor grabbed her attention, a broad smile toying with the curve of his mouth. "With this ring, I thee wed..."

She didn't hear the rest of his words. Tears of joy pricked the back of her eyes. His father had sent the ring. The man must be a messenger from Dunadd. Gregor placed the beautiful gold and peridot ring on the second finger of her left hand.

Deeply touched, Emily stammered through her vows.

"In front of God and these witnesses I proclaim you man and wife. You may kiss your bride, lad," the priest instructed Gregor.

Emily gazed at her new husband with awe. It didn't matter they were strangers. She sensed there was something special between them, perhaps magical, something that bound them together even though they were from different places. Different times.

She studied his full lips, anticipating the feel of them against her mouth. She moistened her lips, wanting him more than she would have imagined possible only a few days prior.

His pupils dilated, and he sucked in a ragged breath. He lifted a loose tendril of her hair and tucked it behind an ear. His calloused fingers brushed along the sensitive skin at the nape of her neck.

Fire and ice. She shivered. A delicious chill tingled over her shoulder blades. Why was he making her wait?

He grasped the back of her neck. Placed his other palm against the curve of her cheek. His hot gaze devoured her. Held her enthralled.

Her pulse quickened. Her mouth went dry.

"Please," she murmured, voice low, raspy, needy.

He grinned and lowered his head. A whisper of breath teased her lips before he made contact and brushed his full lips over hers, the gentle kiss achingly seductive.

She curled her arms around his neck, leaned in, and pressed against his broad chest.

Teasing the seam of her lips, he nudged them apart, deepening the kiss, exploring the moist recesses within, taking possession of her mouth. Of her soul.

She claimed him, too. Chose to forget they stood before those few gathered to witness the wedding.

A loud catcall slipped through the sensual haze surrounding her, and she attempted to pull away. He didn't allow it. His kiss became more demanding, and she surrendered to it. When they finally broke apart, her cheeks flamed with heat.

Holy crap. If he made love the way he kissed, she'd be in heaven.

She kept her thrilled smile to herself as they turned to those who'd come into the small chapel to offer congratulations.

A large ginger-haired man slapped Gregor on the back. "I told you she would take you for a merry ride."

The messenger from Dunadd stepped forward and again hugged Gregor. He then turned to Emily, inquiry in his dark gaze.

"Emily, this is my father. Allain of Dunadd." Gregor pivoted to his father. "My wife, sir."

She should have known. The man's eyes were the same dark chocolate color as his son's. She should have caught the resemblance sooner.

"I am verra pleased to meet you, daughter."

"And I you," she curtsied, guessing that might be

expected.

Isobell scooted over and hugged Emily. "Now we are cousins."

Gregor guided her through the others.

At the doorway, Munn held a jeweled goblet to Emily. Another, he offered to Gregor. "May your marriage be blessed."

Gregor accepted his, but Emily hesitated. Could the contents be tainted by magic?

She glanced over her shoulder to the woman who stood behind her. "Isobell?"

Isobell cast a penetrating stare at the brownie. "May I taste the wine, Munn?"

His wrinkled face wrinkled more, folding in on itself, as he pursed his lips in a nasty grimace. It occurred to Emily the little man was insulted. After a moment more of uncertainty, Munn gave a curt nod.

Isobell accepted the goblet, took a sip, and handed it to Emily. "Quite tasty, my dear. The fruity flavor is verra pleasing. And harmless."

Gregor frowned, glanced at Isobell, and then Emily. He raised a brow.

"I'll explain later," Emily said.

Then she bent her knees and lowered to the brownie's three-foot height. "Thank you for the wine and your heartfelt congratulations." She kissed his cheek.

His unusual blue-green eyes widened. He shuffled his oversized feet and lowered his gaze. Rosy red color suffused his face.

Emily kept a grin to herself as she straightened.

Gregor raised his cup to her, and they shared a wordless glance. Her stomach shimmied with anticipation.

Tevin dashed through the crowd. A stern look from Archie slowed the boy's pace. He wrapped his arms around her legs and looked up at her. "Lady Isobell said I can stay with Lach while you go away. May I? Please?"

Emily had already discussed this with Isobell. She ruffled

his curls. "Sure."

"Come, let us get you changed into something more suitable for riding, Emily." Isobell guided her and Tevin away from the well-wishers.

Allain of Dunadd placed a hand on Gregor's arm as they passed. "May I have a word with you, son? In private?"

Gregor watched the sway of Emily's hips as she withdrew. He raised his cup to the wee brownie. "I thank you for this fine wine, Munn."

He took a long swallow of the ruby liquid then followed his father back through the chapel and into the chief's study. Gregor placed the goblet on the hearth mantle, straightened his shoulders and turned to his sire.

"How did this come about?" Da demanded without preamble.

"By *this*, I assume you refer to my marriage?"

"Aye. What else?" Da's dark eyes smoldered. "I sent you to Castle Lachlan to learn skills from the chief you will require when I am gone and you become keeper at Dunadd. I did not send you here to wed an outlander. I thought you wanted to prove yourself capable?"

"What of my happiness?"

"Ach, Gregor." Da ran a hand through his graying hair. "Of course I want you to be happy, but you have wed a stranger."

"At the command of my chief."

Da's jaw tightened. "Explain."

Gregor retrieved his wine from the hearth and dropped into a chair next to his da. Heavy of heart, he searched his mind for the right words to describe all that transpired since he'd found Emily on the faerie mound.

"Is the *bairn* hers?" Da blurted before Gregor had a chance to form clear thoughts.

"Nae. The lad is the son of Stephen MacEwen."

"Ah…" Da's eyes widened. "Well then, you have quite the tale to tell."

"Aye, sir." Gregor relayed the events leading up to this day.

The chamber became awkwardly silent. Da stood. Paced across the space. He poured some whisky from the flagon the chief kept on a side table into a cup and knocked it back. After another moment passed, he turned and gave Gregor a pointed look. "All I ask is you dinnae consummate your vows so when the threat of danger to the lass and *bairn* has passed you can attain an annulment."

Gregor gulped the remaining wine in his cup, barely tasting its flavor. He had no intention of ending his marriage.

CHAPTER ELEVEN

*E*mily ignored the small pile of clothes on the bed and instead stared at the three knives arranged in an even row on a piece of raw leather. She bit the edge of her lip. "What are those for?"

"Protection." Isobell's matter of fact reply ratcheted up Emily's level of concern.

"I don't have a clue how to use a knife to defend myself or anyone else."

"Of course not. You come from a more civilized time. Gregor will teach you." Isobell placed a hand on Emily's waist, turned her about, and deftly undid the laces on the back of the gown. "Now, let us get you dressed for riding."

"I'm not sure my time is more civilized. There is so much political unrest. Urban riots, hate crimes, terrorist attacks. More and more people carry guns," Emily said, as Isobell dragged an ecru-colored tunic over her head. She squeezed into a pair of tight leather pants. "By the way, whose clothes are these?"

"Mine. I am known for riding about the countryside dressed as a lad."

Emily's eyes popped. "Really?"

"Aye. I like to be comfortable when I ride." Isobell

chuckled.

"I'm so glad. I was afraid I'd have to ride in a dress in order to conform to the local custom." Emily smiled and tugged on her own boots. "Thanks for lending me the clothes."

Isobell rolled the leather cloth around the knives, bound it with a tie, and slipped them into what appeared to be a saddlebag, along with a skirt and another shirt and a chemise. "Gregor can show you where and how to strap the blades to your body." Isobel flexed her eyebrows with exaggeration like Groucho Marx. The woman possessed a contrary mix of past and future idioms.

The craziness of it all helped Emily ignore the heat that flushed her neck and face caused by Isobell's sexual inference. Although, she'd certainly like Gregor to touch several sensitive parts of her body. In only a few hours they would probably make love. The mere thought made her insides clench and her sex weep. What had come over her lately? She'd never gotten all pumped up about sex before. Had she?

Everything seemed so confusing. She rubbed her forehead between her eyes where a slight ache of tension had become a near constant annoyance.

The trip down the circular stairs was much easier in pants and boots. Still, Emily ran a hand along the stone wall as she descended. She met Gregor in the great hall a few moments later.

His eyes lit as she approached. He took the saddlebag from her and placed it on a table behind him alongside another bulging one. Then he turned her about in a circle, his heated gaze sliding over her from head to toe. He leaned in close and whispered in her ear, "You are verra appealing, *wife*, dressed as a lad."

A joyful chuckle bubbled up her throat and escaped from her lips in a burst.

Gregor had donned brown leather pants as well. He wore a hooded rust leather vest over a long sleeved grayish linen shirt. A wide belt clinched a trim waist. On his left forearm was strapped a thick leather arm guard. A sheathed sword hung on his back and a quiver of feathered arrows hung from his hip. He appeared every inch the hunter. She leisurely skimmed his fine physique with a measuring gaze. "Very appealing, indeed, *husband.*"

His cheeks reddened. He actually blushed. His husky chuckle warmed her heart. He twisted his torso toward the table and retrieved her saddlebag along with the other and his bow. "Let us be on our way."

They exited the castle though the courtyard gate and made their way to the pebbly beach where several of those small boats Gregor called *currachs* waited just above the surf.

"Clouds darken the horizon. We should make haste to avoid a soaking." Gregor dropped the saddlebags into one of the boats and dragged it to the water's edge.

She hopped in without getting her feet wet. He wasn't as lucky when he joined her. The view was great. The countryside, of course, but more so, the flex of masculine muscle, fabric taut, with each tug on the oars.

After a short hike up the hill to the stables, Gregor assisted Emily into the saddle of a chestnut mare. He seemed awkward. His hands displayed a slight tremble. He stumbled when he attempted to mount his horse.

"Are you all right?" she asked. He seemed disoriented.

"I am fine," he claimed as he rose to the saddle and took his seat. She wasn't sure she believed him. He looked a bit green about the gills.

"Are you sure you want to ride out today? We could wait and go tomorrow after a good night's sleep."

He grinned. "I dinnae plan to get much sleep this night."

She glanced away to hide her burning face. Heated cheeks were becoming way too common of late.

They climbed to the ridge above the stables and followed the tree line. Long-haired cattle grazed the grasses along the slope below. After a distance, they entered a narrow trail, riding in single file—Emily tailed Gregor—in silence. The soft purring trills and high see-see-sees of crested tits accompanied them along the woodsy track. Occasionally, Emily caught glimpses of the small grayish birds and another yellow variety she didn't know by name.

They'd ridden for what seemed like an hour when Gregor started to whistle a not quite rhythmic tune and sway in the saddle.

What on earth? Emily tightened the distance between them, concerned by his strange behavior. When the trail widened, she rode up alongside. He glanced over and gave her a shit-eating grin. His glassy eyes darting about. Was he drunk?

"Gregor?"

"Just a wee farther," he said, the words somewhat slurred.

They broke from the trees into a large meadow. Before she could say another word, he urged his horse to go faster and took off across the grassy field dappled by yellow blooms.

Shit! She pressed her horse to keep pace.

He slowed at the opposite side and, one after the other, they entered another wooded trail, the scent of fir heavy in the humid air. He kept a horse length in front of her not allowing her to catch up.

After riding another mile or so, they entered a clearing that encircled a thatched roofed stone cottage and a smaller wattle and daub structure. Lightning streaked the distant sky. Thunder resounded over the mountains.

Emily slid from her horse with only a slight leg wobble when she landed. She approached Gregor. He was slower at dismounting. His legs faltered upon hitting the hard ground, and he leaned on the horse, hanging onto the saddle for support.

"I dinnae feel well," he said in a weak voice.

"Are you drunk? Were you drinking the whole time while I changed out of my wedding gown?" She couldn't keep the annoyance from her voice.

"Nae." He pushed away from the animal. "Only had that

one goblet of wine…"

"From Munn," they said in unison.

"The wee scunner must have played me a *pliskie*."

"A what?"

"Trick." He waved an arm and nearly toppled over. "Prank."

"But why?"

"That I dinnae ken."

The wind kicked up. The uppermost branches of the tallest firs waved with a buzzy whisper. A burst blew through the clearing. Dried leaves tumbled across the ground, tip over stem. Branches of a mighty oak rustled. In the following calm, the smell of ozone seasoned the air.

"It's about to rain. Let's get you inside then I'll care for the horses. I'll carry the saddlebags. You take your weapons." She had no desire to touch those.

"I can help with the bags." He staggered.

"No. You go in the cottage."

A gust of wind grabbed hold of the wood as she opened the door. The heavy oak slammed against the inside wall with an echoing thump. She tossed the saddlebags on the floor and shoved Gregor hard to get him to move.

His shoulders slumped, but he conceded. "Bed the horses in the wee hut."

After the door shut behind Gregor, she coaxed the skittish animals through the wind that now blasted the clearing like a speeding freight train with no conductor to slow it down. The hut was better built than she first supposed. Someone had recently been there; fresh hay covered the dirt floor and leather bags containing oats hung from two posts. Emily tied the reins of each horse to a different post then removed the saddles and rubbed down the animals with a cloth she found with other supplies on a shelf.

Thin fissures in the walls hummed from the onslaught of wind. She'd wait until after the storm passed to give the animals a good grooming. Hair whipped her face, getting caught in her eyes and mouth as she fought the wind on the trip back to the cottage. Steps from the door, rain pelted the ground in a loud whish of sound.

Emily dashed for the door. Once inside, she leaned against the closed panel and heaved a hearty sigh. Then her eyes popped as she took in the interior of the cottage. Rustic, but not. Someone had visited before them, making the space a romantic haven from the storm. "Wow. Who did this?"

Body hunched, head bowed into hands, Gregor sat on a bed in the corner of the single room. The mattress had been dressed with the finest of silks and velvets and furs. He appeared so masculine sitting within what had obviously been meant as a love nest. His gaze slowly rose to hers. His complexion really did look green in the dim light.

"'Tis the chief's hunting lodge. Though he spends more time here with his lady-wife than hunting. Lady Isobell likes her comfort. She must have sent a couple of her women and a lad or two. She wanted to make our eve'n special."

Emily stepped to the center of the room to warm chilled hands at the small fire burning in a pit of sorts. A spiral of sweet-scented wood smoke rose, sucked out through a hole in the ceiling. She flicked her gaze to where a couple braces of lit candles in iron holders sat atop a rough-hewn table covered by an embroidered ecru linen cloth. A platter of cheese and apples sat upon the table as well as a couple of platters covered with linen cloths.

An equally rough wooden bench topped by a purple velvet cushion sat in front of a shuttered window that held back the fierceness of the storm, making the quaint room a cozy haven.

She approached Gregor and knelt on the woven rush mat in front of him. "Your words aren't as slurred as earlier, how do you feel?"

"Like I was kicked in the gut by an angry horse."

"Maybe you should eat something. We've been provided with a fine feast."

If at all possible, he turned a deeper shade of ill. "Need sleep."

He dragged his legs onto the bed, rolled over, and passed out. At least he'd removed his sword and quiver before she'd returned. They were on the floor beside the bed with his bow and boots.

What was she to do? She glanced at the buffet on the table. No. She wasn't hungry.

She retrieved the chemise from her saddlebag, stripped off her clothes, and donned the thin linen slip. She bit her lip, uncertain. Oh screw it. She climbed into bed next to him and spooned against his back.

Emotion swamped her. This felt nice. Like when she'd slept with—

The pang of pain hit her right between the eyes. She lay there, unmoving, praying for the headache to recede.

A few hours later, Emily startled awake. Gregor still slept soundly. She padded across the floor.

She pulled open the door and stood in the opening, gazing out into the evening. The storm was long gone, but an eerie mist had laid claim to the land beyond the cottage. A chill snaked over her shoulder blades, and she shivered. Was there someone out there watching from within the thick haze?

Get a grip, Emily. Maybe she wasn't comfortable alone in the wilderness because she had little experience with such. She glanced back at the bed where Gregor slept the sleep of the drugged. When he woke she'd ask him to teach her how to use the knives.

She wrapped her arms over her chest. Considering her recent experience with the mist's hidden dangers, more than likely she'd overreacted. For Pete's sake, who in their right mind would have thought there was an enchanted time gate in the woods behind a garden center in Anderson Creek? Emily shut the door and returned to the bed.

Gregor used a dream-hewed blade to slice through the thick, ropelike web wound about his body as he held the menacing six-eyed stare of the hairy spider keeping him prisoner within the realm of sleep. Unfettered, he jolted awake, eyes opening wide. His heart thundered within his chest as it had when he'd chased the white stag onto the *Sithichean Sluaigh*.

He remained still, unclear of his surroundings. After several tense moments, his mind rose above the nightmarish muck of his drugged slumber, and he remembered riding to the chief's hunting lodge with...*Emily*.

He rolled to the side.

She slept beside him atop the covers, her thin chemise hiked to her waist, exposing to his hungry gaze a nicely rounded feminine arse. He hardened at the sight.

Christ! He wore no garment. He must have risen from the bed at some point and cast his clothing aside, for the lass couldn't have undressed him.

He slid his gaze over Emily's lovely curves to her face. Dark lashes shadowed high cheekbones. Creamy ivory skin bore a pinkish blush, perhaps from the sun, or from the exertion of the ride to the lodge or from the wind. Sweetly bowed rosy lips made him want to kiss her awake.

Awed by her beauty, he drew in a ragged breath. In distraction, he swept a trembling finger along the smooth length of a muscular feminine leg.

The cadence of her breathing changed. Her eyes fluttered open. "Oh, hey."

"Good eve'n, lass."

She snuggled close, rubbed against his rigid arousal, killed him with burgeoning desire.

He cleared a suddenly dry throat. "I agreed to wed with you, be it in name only, or more, to protect you and the wee lad. I want the more. What say you?"

She placed a finger to his lips. "Don't talk. Just kiss me."

That was the only encouragement needed. He dragged her sideways over his body. Touched her lips softly with his, a mere whisper of a touch, then more fiercely, wanting, needing her taste in his mouth.

CHAPTER TWELVE

*G*regor dropped Emily's discarded chemise over the side of the bed onto the floor, holding her close, glorying in the sensual slide of skin against skin. "Ach, lass. You feel good in my arms."

"I like being in your arms." She chuckled and rose over him.

Their gazes met, lingered. Mutual desire acknowledged without words.

He kissed her lips, her face, the hollow of her throat.

She licked the contour of his ear, blew into it. Made him shiver with delight. She nibbled the lobe. Drove him near to the edge of endurance. Heat pulsed through his blood. He growled and rolled her beneath him. He wanted to devour every bit of her.

Gregor laved a rosy nipple. Blew on the tip. Made her flesh pucker and tighten into a hard bud. He sucked it into his mouth, swirled his tongue around the taut tip, and savored the moans escaping her throat. Needing more, needing all of her, he tended to her other breast with the same thorough devotion.

She grabbed fistfuls of his hair. "Please, Gregor," she said, urging him onward.

"Everything for you." He used his teeth, a gentle bite. She panted and bucked against him. "Easy." He didn't know if he murmured the word for her benefit or his. His arousal had hardened to near pain. Pleasure-pain. He was breathing hard. He needed to slow down or he would spend his seed too soon.

He untangled her hands from his hair and yanked his head from her grasp, ignoring the sting to his scalp. He resumed worshiping her pert breasts.

She panted and gripped the bed covering. "Gregor, you're driving me insane."

A smile teased his lips, and he released the nipple from his mouth. "We have only just begun."

He splayed his hands on the curve of her hips, holding her in place, using his lips to leisurely wander over her flat belly, cherishing her with soft kisses. When he reached the curls of her mons, he inhaled sharply, taking in her scent. He drew the womanly fragrance deep into his nostrils, and his erection kicked.

His pleasure must wait. He would see Emily satisfied first.

She rose onto her elbows, her hair disheveled, her brown eyes glazed with passion. "I want you inside me. Now."

"Soon, sweetling." Holding her gaze, he stuck a finger into his mouth, wet it, and ever so slowly withdrew it, popping it out. Her eyes flared.

He bowed his head and teased the folds at the entrance to her sex with the moisture on his finger. Emily dropped back to the mattress, allowing him to delve deeper. When he stroked the nub within, she undulated and cried out. She would scream his name in ecstasy before they were through.

He replaced his finger with his tongue and worked her without mercy, her taut body open to him. She came into his mouth with a roar, and he swallowed her flavor, relishing the lingering taste on his lips.

"Holy crap, Gregor." She went limp. "You *are* amazing."

"We are not done." He could wait no longer. He stalked up her length and cradled his cock between her thighs. With a swift thrust, his stiff erection was sheathed to the hilt within her heat. She wrapped her legs around his waist and rocked. Their gazes met and held. Sensation tingled along his length. He withdrew from her warmth and thrust again. They fell into a rhythm. Emily giving, him taking. He giving, she taking. The pressure built, the pleasure burned, and united as one they exploded in a burst of vibrant color. She screamed his name. He yelled hers.

As the euphoria ebbed, Gregor held Emily snug within loving arms. They fit perfectly together. He felt the cadence of her heart as if it belonged to him. Two hearts thundering as one. He would never let her go.

Emily luxuriated within a haze of pleasure. Warm air wafted through the open window, teasing her bare skin. At some point during the night, Gregor had risen to check on the horses and opened the shutter before returning to bed and making love to her for the third or fourth time. Who was counting? She raised her arms over her head in a languid stretch.

Gregor's ragged intake of breath made her smile.

"You steal my breath, lass."

She rolled onto her side and ran a finger along the length of his thigh. His cock jerked. She smiled and moistened her lips.

"If you gaze at me like that for much longer, the sun will be high in the sky before we break our fast."

"And just how am I gazing at you?"

"Like you want to eat me alive."

"So I do." She grasped the length of his erection and caressed him from tip to hilt. Emily liked the feel of him—akin to stroking a soft chamois cloth over a hard steel rod.

His head dropped to the pillow on a heavy exhale. "Grrrrrh!"

She giggled. She couldn't help it. It was so much fun to play with him.

In a swift move, she replaced her hand with her mouth.

She sucked his cock, using her tongue to circle the tip, especially the spot she somehow knew to be especially sensitive. His groin rose off the bed, and he fisted the sheeting at his sides. He said something, the words nothing more than gibberish.

She continued to work him. Licking. Sucking. Drawing him deep. The muscles in his neck went taut. His face reddened and sweat bloomed across his forehead. She didn't let up until his cum surged into her mouth. She swallowed. Sucked him dry. Then ran her tongue over her lips, loving his taste.

"Come here. Let me hold you." Several minutes passed before he managed to utter those coherent words.

Emily slid into the crook of his arm, pillowed her head on his pec. And so they stayed in comfortable silence until her stomach growled.

Gregor chuckled. "We must feed you."

He handed her the chemise from the floor then grabbed a plaid from the bed and wrapped it about his waist. Damn. He looked good dressed like a Highlander—as if he'd jumped off the cover of a romance novel. Calves firm. Long hair draping drool-worthy muscles covering his broad chest and strong arms.

Lowering her gaze before he caught her ogling his assets, she slipped on the chemise and donned the skirt and tunic Isobell had so thoughtfully provided.

Tee teehee hee.

"Shite! Those blasted pixies are back," Gregor barked.

Emily joined him at the table. Sure enough, the lavender-winged pixie perched on the rim of a tall cup. Two others flitted about, darting to and fro over the platters of food.

Gregor picked up the mug and held it in front of his face. "What do you want, wee lass?"

The pixie withdrew a fist from behind her back and tossed a white powder into his face. He coughed and dropped the cup to the table. He swiped at his eyes.

The pixie had fallen into the mug. She grasped the edge

and shimmied over the side.

"Begone." Gregor shooed her away with an abrupt wave of his arm.

Tee teehee hee. Tee teehee hee. The other pixies tittered.

The green pixie flew at Emily, hovering inches from her face, peridot wings vigorously fluttering like those of a hummingbird. She held her diminutive hand to her mouth and, palm open, spewed the same fine powder on a wisp of released breath into Emily's face.

Emily blinked. "Why do they keep doing that?"

The three pixies darted out of the window.

Gregor dropped to the bench and laughed. "To retain their reputation for being pesky."

Emily joined him in his mirth, laughing until her sides ached.

"Shall we have something to eat?" She sat beside him and wiped tears from her eyes.

"Aye. I find I am quite hungry, wife. You ken I had a busy night."

She felt a blush stain her cheeks, but didn't linger on the embarrassment. She'd enjoyed every moment of their busy night.

They shared heather ale and bannocks splattered with honey.

"I thought to go hunting for a wee and set a few snares within the wood. Perhaps we will have rabbit stew for our eve'n meal."

She'd never eaten rabbit, but she was game. "Okay." she said. "One of these platters is full of vegetables."

"Isobell foresaw our every need." He changed into his leathers, strapped a knife to his calf, two others disappeared up his sleeves.

So that is what I'm supposed to do with the knives Isobell forced on me.

Gregor dropped a quick kiss on her forehead and grabbed his bow and arrows. "I will return shortly."

Several hours later, Emily paced the small space from the table to the bed, her cheeks hot with thoughts of what they had done on that mattress throughout the night. Gregor turned out to be an amazing lover as she'd suspected after their first kiss. She sighed.

Then her memory flicked to another time, to another lover. Laughing black eyes. Jet black hair. She rubbed suddenly aching temples.

What had she been thinking?

Emily tramped back to the table, confusion wrinkling her forehead. She looked out the unshuttered window, unseeing. A roll of the neck did little to ease the building anxiety. The walls seemed to crowd in on her.

She rushed to the door and stepped outside. Golden sunshine hit her face, chasing away some of the mind-numbing angst. Emily inhaled the sharp pitch of sun-warmed evergreens. Took note of the dark green fir trees contrasting beautifully with the pure blue of the sky. She shook her head, feeling foolish. Her unease was nothing more than being left alone in an unfamiliar place. She missed Gregor. What should she do until he returned?

Emily strolled around to the side of the cottage to where a rough wooden bench had been placed in the shade. After she'd sat there for the better part of an hour, her skin prickled with goose bumps. She jerked her gaze around the clearing trying to see beyond the open space and into the shadowy realm of the trees. Was she being watched?

A flash of white darted through the trees. The rustling of branches followed. Was someone there?

She leapt from the bench and ran for the door of the cottage. Gregor had left behind his sword. She had the leather-bound knives. Certainly, she could use them for protection if there was a threat.

Before she made it through the door, an arm shot out and grabbed her. She shrieked.

"Easy, lass. I did not mean to frighten you."

"Gregor! You scared the shit out of me."

He wrapped his arms around her. "Your heart is racing, sweetling. Are you unwell?"

"I glimpsed a white flash in the woods."

"Aye. I saw deer tracks. I imagine the white stag is in the area. The one I was aiming at when the pixie startled my shot and my arrow grazed you."

"I thought someone was spying on me." She shrugged a shoulder. "Foolish. I know."

"Nae. You need to be aware of your surroundings."

"Did you see any other tracks? Maybe there is another hunter in the woods."

Gregor rubbed his chin and frowned. "'Tis possible someone else tracks the beast."

"You seem disappointed."

"Ach, well." He dragged a hand through his hair. "Come. Sit with me and I will explain."

"What is it?" She grasped his hand after they sat together on the outside bench. "Is something wrong?"

"When I fostered at Castle Lachlan in my youth I acted as a reckless lad. Always in trouble. My chief and my father fretted I would never learn the discipline required to take my father's place when he relinquishes the keepership of Dunadd."

"Are you the oldest child?"

"Nae. I have two older sisters. But I am the only son. Therefore, my father's heir."

"I see."

"You sound like you disapprove."

"Things are different in the place from where I come. A female can inherit, same as a male."

"There have been occurrences within the realm where a woman was placed into leadership, but 'tis uncommon." Gregor smiled, but sounded skeptical of the merit. "I had hoped this time, during my tenure at Castle Lachlan, I would prove myself worthy to the clan, to my chief, to my father."

"And to yourself?"

"Aye."

"You thought to prove your worth by bringing in the white stag."

He gave an abrupt nod.

"Instead you brought me to their door—a problem."

"I dinnae regret it." He squeezed her hand. "I dinnae regret it at all."

CHAPTER THIRTEEN

Their idyllic time at the hunting lodge passed too quickly. Emily glanced over a shoulder at the stone structure one last time before urging the chestnut mare to follow Gregor's horse onto the trail through the trees.

They traversed the same track they'd traveled several days earlier in the reverse direction. Just before they would have ridden from the woods into the large meadow, Gregor held out a hand, motioning for her to halt.

"What is it?" she asked.

"A large party of riders cross from the Dunoon overland trail headed toward the Loch Fyne trail. Same as us. Few from this part of Scotland can afford to ride in such numbers. 'Tis either the Earl of Argyll, chief of Clan Campbell, or Ninian Stewart, the Sheriff of Bute."

"Surely not the sheriff." Emily's pulse rate spiked. Considering Isobell's description, the sheriff was the last person she wished to meet. "Do you think they are looking for me? For Tevin?"

"Easy, lass. We dinnae ken if it is the sheriff. However, we will let them pass before proceeding."

They waited in silence while the riders crossed the meadow in a canter, their forms appearing smaller and smaller until completely disappearing upon entering the trail into the woods on the far side of the meadow. Emily and Gregor waited another twenty minutes before crossing the field of summer grass and yellow gorse. For the next hour or so, they kept to a slower pace, not wishing to overtake the larger party.

At the loch end of the trail, they lingered, watching the other riders from within the concealment of the trees instead of riding out onto the wide-open ridge above Loch Fyne.

"We are in luck, lass," Gregor said. "They turn east toward Campbell country, away from Castle Lachlan."

Emily released a heavy sigh of relief, her heart rate at last slowing to a normal beat.

Gregor leaned toward her, grasped her hand, and gave it a gentle squeeze. At the snap of a branch, his gaze jerked beyond her to the woods behind. His eyes narrowed, his stare fixated. "Dinnae move."

"What is it?" she asked.

"The white stag," he whispered in an awed voice.

In the distance she faced, farther down the slope, golden sunlight shimmered on the surface of the water surrounding Castle Lachlan in welcome.

"Go. Hunt your stag. The stables and castle are within sight. I'll be perfectly safe continuing on alone."

"You are sure?"

"Absolutely. Go. Give it your best shot." She winked at him.

"I will return before nightfall."

Emily watched him ride off. She bit the edge of her lip. Worry furrowed her brow. He was too obsessed with that damn white stag. Too obsessed with trying to prove himself to everyone. She supposed it was the way of men, especially in this time period.

With a click of her tongue against her teeth, she reined the mare toward the distant stables, following the tree line along the ridge. The animal faltered mid-stride in a patch of tall grass and Emily barely kept her seat. She patted its neck and murmured calming words. The mare emitted a loud nasal snort then took a couple of steps. The poor animal walked with a pronounced limp.

Craptastic! The horse was lame.

Emily slid from the saddle to the ground and squatted to check the animal's foreleg. She didn't see anything wrong. Perhaps the horse pulled a muscle or tore a tendon. She'd have to walk it on lead to the stables. Emily stood and a large hand clamped over her mouth from behind, muffling her scream, the point of some sort of blade pressed beneath her left rib.

"Dinnae holler, and I will not harm ye," snarled a hoarse male voice near her ear.

She gave an abrupt nod. Panic heaved bile up her throat, the taste sour in her mouth.

He removed the hand silencing her, but used the appendage to hold her trapped, her back pressed against a sturdy chest.

"Ye will come with me. The *bairn*, Tevin, has a need of ye."

"Where is he?" she demanded, not that she could do anything if the man refused to answer. Tevin should be safe at the castle, playing with his new friend Lach.

She glanced at the saddlebag hanging on her horse, to the pocket that contained the knives she'd yet to touch. If only she'd asked Gregor to show her how to strap them on and use them, she'd have a blade up her sleeve at this very moment to use in defense. "Please, tell me where he is," she said, in a more cajoling voice.

"Hunting dragons with my brother. The lad has been askin' for ye."

Why would Tevin have gone with a stranger? *It's my destiny to kill an orange dragon.*

She flicked her gaze to the stables farther along the ridge. It was too distant for anyone there to hear a yell for help. Only the nearby long-haired cows chewing cud would hear her scream. She really didn't have many options. She'd need to go with him. "Who are you?"

"Will ye come along with nae trouble?"

"Do I have a choice?"

"Ye can come with me freely, or I will thump ye on the noggin and tie ye over the rump of my horse. Matters little to me."

"I will come with you."

"Wise lass." He released her and stepped back. "Turn around slowly."

She spun about instead and pinned a stocky blond-haired man—a man who looked somewhat familiar—with a hard glare. Then it occurred to her. "You're Ciaran's brother."

"What of it?"

Ciaran must have lured Tevin away from the castle with the tale of dragons. But why?

"Where is Tevin? Is he hurt?"

"The lad talks too much, but he remains unharmed."

"Why—"

"Nae more questions. We go now."

"My horse is lame."

"Then ye will ride with me." He grabbed her arm and tugged, dragging her into the woods.

She glanced at the saddlebag again. Too late now. She'd have to go with him.

Hidden from the view of others, concealed by a screen of large bushes and small trees, he mounted a large black horse and yanked her up behind him. His body odor swamped her sinuses and made her want to gag. He stayed within the trees as they rode away from Castle Lachlan and the only people she knew in Scotland circa 1521.

"What is your name?" she asked after they'd been riding for a while.

"Cinead." That was all he said for the rest of the journey.

The man didn't seem to mind her observing the ground they covered and marking the way in her mind. Either they weren't concerned she'd escape and bring others against them, or they had no intention of letting her leave alive.

But why had they taken Tevin and now her?

They rode for the better part of the afternoon. As the sun set, they crossed a stream, or what Gregor would call a burn. Gosh, she missed him. What would he think when he didn't find her at the castle? Would he come after her?

When Emily finally slid off the horse, she was chilled and ached everywhere. She'd love to curl up and go to sleep, but needed to keep her wits about her. She had a feeling that both hers and Tevin's lives were at risk.

"Where are we?" she demanded, again, as if she had some measure of control.

Her captor said nothing. He went about the business of removing branches, still green with leaves, from where they camouflaged the mouth of a cave.

Emily shuddered. She hated dark, tight places.

Cinead lit a torch. "Come. The lad is within."

She clamped down on escalating panic and followed him into the cavernous space that narrowed and split.

"Finally. You have brought her." Ciaran strode from the darkness and grabbed her arm in a painful grip. He dragged her farther into the abyss and shoved her into another smaller chamber within the network of caverns. "Now care for the *bairn*."

Tevin sat on a bed of sorts. He raised a tearstained face. "Em!"

"Oh, sweetheart, are you okay?"

The child lunged for her, wrapped his thin arms around her legs, and sobbed.

The sound broke her heart. She lowered into a squat and hugged him. "Did they hurt you?"

He shook his head. "The pixies were here. The one with the blue wings told me not to cry. She said you and Gregor would come for me. But I couldn't stop crying. I'm sorry."

"It's okay, Tev. I'm here now."

"Where's Gregor?"

"He'll come." She prayed for her words to be true.

She picked up Tevin and hugged him close, then returned

to the outer chamber. "I don't understand," she said to Ciaran and his brother. "Why are you keeping us prisoner?"

Ciaran glared at Tevin. "Because his father is responsible for our *dear* sister's death."

"Maybe we should let them go," Cinead suggested. "'Tisn't like we can keep them, and we cannot kill them. Can we?"

Shit. These men were crazy. Emily's heart dropped to the bottom of her stomach. *Please Gregor. Come for us.* If he didn't, she didn't want to imagine what would happen to her and Tevin.

Gregor had stalked the white stag a distance from where he left his horse when the hairs on the back of his neck stood on end. An uneasy dread settled in his gut. He scanned his surroundings. Afternoon waned. Shadows darkened the wood. He sensed he wasn't alone.

He held his bow in a taut grip.

A sudden breeze blew through the trees, rustling leaves, and within its breath buzzed three pixies. The lavender pixie flew in close, hovered in front of his face, and blew dust in his face, again, then backed away quick. *Tee teehee hee.*

Gregor swatted at her. He didn't want to hurt her, just wanted her to leave him alone.

She landed on his shoulder, grasped wee handfuls of his hair and, with a flutter of wings, yanked. He shook his head. She lost her hold, fell to his shoulder on her rump, tumbled backwards twice, and then lifted into the air.

The other two pixies snickered then joined the assault. All three wee creatures flew at him, each grabbing hair and pulling as if to draw him in the opposite direction from that taken by the white stag.

"Stop it!" he shouted, annoyance making his voice harsh. He attempted to fend them off without hurting them, but after several minutes, he gave in. "All right. What is it you want?"

One flew backwards, waving an arm for him to follow. The other two joined the first. He nodded and followed their erratic flight through the wood to...

His horse grazed sparse grass in the shade of an oak exactly where he staked the beast. If he hurried, they'd arrive home as the hour before gloaming shadowed the land.

Tee teehee hee. Tee teehee hee.

The pixies giggled then vanished as if they'd never been there.

He must be daft to trust the fae pixies. Gregor grimaced and straddled his horse. He reined the animal homeward. Clearing the wood, he rode along the ridge headed for the stable, beyond exhausted, eager for a hot bath, hot meal, and an eve'n within his wife's warm embrace. When he rode into the stable yard, he found the chief and his *lèine-chneas* gathered, preparing to mount.

"Tevin has gone missing," the chief exclaimed. "Lach admitted having learned in confidence that the wee lad set off with Ciaran. Stephen's *bairn* believes they travel to Ben Nevis to hunt dragons. I doubt they have traveled to the mountain. My guess is Ciaran has something more nefarious planned, and closer to home." The chief glanced past Gregor. "Where is Emily?"

"We parted where the woodland trail meets the ridge. She was to head directly to the stables and Castle Lachlan while I stalked the white stag. Did she not arrive at the keep?"

"Lad, did Mistress Emily return her mount?" the chief asked of a passing stable lad.

"Nae, sir. The horse wandered in alone, and lame. I have not seen the lady."

"Why was I not informed?" he blustered. "Never mind. Bring a fresh mount for Gregor."

Stunned by the news, Gregor stood still as stone. *What the hell happened to Emily?*

CHAPTER FOURTEEN

Well past sunset, they still hadn't found tracks indicating which direction Ciaran had taken Tevin, or Emily had gone. Darkness had since claimed the land, and the scouts sought a spot to camp for the night. Gregor didn't want to halt the search. He dreaded speculating on what could happen to his wife and the *bairn* overnight. He suspected Ciaran had kidnapped them both. What could be the man's motive?

Surrounded by torchbearers, Gregor rode between the chief and Duncan, and amidst others of their kin. He rubbed his tight chest. Fear threatened to overwhelm him. Suddenly, three hovering, sparkling lights appeared in front of the group of MacLachlan warriors. One blue, one green, and one lavender with purple swirls. The lavender separated from the others and wove its way through the riders, buzzing his cheek in passing.

During the quick encounter, he caught a glimpse of the ebony-haired, winged lass within the star-like surge of light. "Damned pixies."

Would he never be free of the wee creatures?

Tee teehee hee. She circled the chief before rejoining her brethren.

"I believe she wants us to follow," the chief said with a

chuckle, seeming more pleased than Gregor would have imagined. "Perhaps they will lead us to Emily and Tevin."

More colorful lights—representing all the varied hues of a rainbow—joined the original three. The pixies flew in an undulating pattern, creating a wave-shaped path of light. Beacons in the night.

"Dim your torches, lads. We follow the pixies," the chief ordered. The man was more trusting of Fae magic than Gregor, but at least they weren't abandoning the search to sleep.

They rode through the dark of the new moon, guided by the pixie light. Hope replaced fear in Gregor's heart.

By dawn's earliest radiance the pixies left them to their own devices, and the party of men crossed a shallow burn in single file. On the opposite shore, they followed its flow south until Duncan stopped and leaned over the side of his horse.

"Tracks!" he called over a shoulder.

Gregor leapt from his mount and squatted on the ground. He touched the distinct mark of a horse hoof in the mud. "Probably fresh from yestereve," he reported. "'Tis deep, as if the beast carries more than one rider."

One of the riders might be Emily. He strode farther afield, combing through undergrowth, eyes peeled for another sign, his abrupt actions driven by hopeful impatience.

The other men fanned out in silence. After a short time, Duncan waved Gregor over to a boggy area where the big man searched the ground. He indicated another impression in the mud. "They traveled this way."

Reins in hand, the men followed the tracks on foot, led by the chief and Duncan.

Duncan fell back and into pace next to Gregor. "Dinnae be disappointed if this rider is not the one. We will find the lass and the wee lad."

Gregor swallowed uneasily. The longer the two were missing, the harder it would be to find them. Anything could happen to a lone woman and *bairn* out in this wilderness.

The chief, using hand motions, signaled for them to stop. Footsteps marked the dusty dirt. Many large like men's, a few smaller like a woman's, and some *bairn* sized. One of the men pointed to a pile of loose brush. On closer inspection, they discovered a mouth to a cave.

With a tilt of the head and more hand signals, the chief commanded them to back off and find defensive positions. Gregor followed the order with reluctance. Emily was his wife. He should be the one to draw out whoever was in that cave. He nocked an arrow to his raised bow and drew it back to his jaw. His gaze followed the length of the shaft, his aim on the mouth of the cave. He waited, his nerves as taut as the bow string.

Duncan conferred with the chief off to the side of the cave mouth. He signaled for two of the men to follow him into the cave. 'Twas torture not to be one of those to enter. Gregor wanted to be the man to find his wife.

After what felt like an eternity, the three backed out of the cave, arms raised to the side, away from their weapons in concession. Ciaran exited next, Emily held in front of him, trapped by a meaty arm. In his other hand, he wielded a blade. His brother attempted to contain a squirming Tevin, who bit the man's hand at the same time as Emily kicked back, her foot connecting with her captor's balls. They broke free amid a hail of foul swearing and startled *ooofs*. Duncan grabbed Tevin and carried the lad to safety.

Without conscious thought, Gregor released the primed arrow into Cinead's throat. Blood gurgled from the man's mouth as he fell to the ground.

Gregor dropped the bow and lunged forward, but stopped short.

Ciaran had somehow regained control of Emily and now held the blade to her throat. "If you want the lass, give me the lad in exchange."

The chief stepped forward. "Why do you want the *bairn?*"

"I am owed," Ciaran claimed. "MacEwen murdered my sister."

"You ken that is not the truth. Malcolm Maclay murdered your sister."

"MacEwen kilt her even if he was not the one who beat her to death."

While the discourse continued, Gregor retrieved his bow and nocked another arrow, but couldn't take a shot at Ciaran without risking Emily.

Ciaran glanced at his brother, dead on the ground. His gaze swung to Gregor then to the chief. "If you wish to negotiate the release of this woman, call off your bowman."

"'Tis his wife you threaten."

"Call him off."

"Stand down, Gregor."

Gregor lowered the bow and arrow, but didn't relax his stance.

The discussion dragged on with unreasonable requests from Ciaran. Refusals from the chief.

"If I release the lass, you will allow me to leave a free man," Ciaran pressed.

"You ken I cannot allow such without"—the chief held the man's stare—"trial by combat."

"Aye," Ciaran agreed and tossed Emily aside.

She stumbled across the distance between her and Gregor and fell into his embrace. She quaked within his arms. He kissed her hair, her face, her lips. He held her tight, hoping to chase away some of the horror of her ordeal.

"Choose your weapon, lad," the chief's voice boomed.

Ciaran lunged behind a large rock and, rising with a claymore in his hand, moved into a defensive position.

"So be it." The chief directed an abrupt nod to Duncan.

The big man pulled his claymore from the sheath strapped to his back and took a fighting stance opposite the other warrior.

"Nae," Gregor bellowed. "He abducted my wife. 'Tis my right to do battle with the villain."

"As you wish." The chief inclined his head.

"Don't do anything crazy on my account." Emily gripped

Gregor's wrist. "I couldn't live with myself if you were harmed, or worse."

"Dinnae ever again insult my manhood, my honor, in such a public display," he said in a low growl meant only for Emily's ears. She cringed away from him, eyes wide. He handed her off to another of the MacLachlan warriors. "Keep her safe."

Gregor gripped the cold steel of the two-handed sword as he would an axe. The claymore was not his best weapon. He clenched his jaw. Anger at the doubt Emily held of his abilities burned in his gut. He needed to harvest that rage and direct it at his adversary. The man had dared take what belonged to him.

In a fluid motion, Gregor stepped forward with his lead foot, his sword stretched out in front of his torso, blade in a diagonal position, cross guard held high, tip pointed slightly back, and faced his opponent.

Ciaran circled, and Gregor followed his movement. The man attacked.

Gregor warded the blow with the flat of his blade, close to the hilt, diminishing the power of the strike. Using his sword and body as one, he counterattacked. With the clang of steel against steel, the blow hit the other sword in time with the motion of his hips and the completion of his step, jarring the length of his arm.

Ciaran backed away, circled again.

Strike following strike, blow following blow, one attacking and one defending, the fight continued.

Weariness took its toll. Gregor must end this, and quick.

Their blades crossed. Gregor released one hand from his sword and gripped the hilt of Ciaran's sword between the man's hands, slipped a foot behind his leg, and forced him down to the ground. In a follow-through, the point of Gregor's sword pricked the man's throat, and with just the right amount of pressure drew a few drops of blood that ran down the man's neck. "Yield?"

"Never."

The chief gave Gregor an abrupt nod.

With no other choice, he twisted his grip on the sword, applied force, and pierced the man's jugular. Hot blood spurted up Gregor's arm and a metallic scent affronted his nostrils, as the other man's life bled away.

He dropped the sword to the ground. Bent over, hands on knees, and gulped large quantities of air. When he raised his head, his gaze found Emily within the crowd. She held her stomach as if in pain. Her lips were pressed tight in disapproval. Her gaze condemning. She looked upon him as if he were the devil incarnate. Her horrified expression sliced him to the core.

Gregor straightened to his full height. Would she forgive him?

CHAPTER FIFTEEN

Warm morning sunlight kissed Emily's face, but she couldn't shake a bone-deep chill.

Tevin broke away from the grasp of the warrior who'd held him back during the fight, and leapt into Emily's open arms. She hugged him close and dropped her head to his soft curls. The boy was so young. He shouldn't have witnessed what just happened. *She* shouldn't have had to witness the bloody execution of two men. Both condemned to death by Gregor's weapons.

Had this been another attempt to prove himself to his father, to his chief, to his clan?

Emily could barely look at him. What he had done was barbaric. His world was violent and cruel. And his anger before the fight had been directed at her, when all she'd wanted was for him to remain safe. She couldn't continue with their farce of a marriage. She couldn't stay in this brutal land.

Astonished gasps from those surrounding her made Emily glance up.

A human-sized, green glow shimmered at the edge of the trees across the clearing from the cave. Emily stared, mesmerized. As the luminescence faded, a tall willowy

woman with fiery auburn hair appeared from within. Her
gauzy green gown was sashed with green and purple tartan
fabric clasped at the shoulder with a gold brooch intricately
crafted with thistle designs and amethyst gemstones. A
brooch Emily had seen on multiple occasions at the
Whispering Pines Inn.

Ohmygod! Caitrina.

How did she get here?

Archie strode forward, Duncan and Gregor flanking him.
They bowed before Caitrina as if she were royalty rather than
the owner of a garden center in Anderson Creek.

"'Tis grand to greet you again, my lady." Archie kissed the
tips of her fingers. "To what do we owe your visit?"

"Munn tells me the pixie clan is causing havoc again."

"Aye. They brought Stephen's *bairn* and Emily through
the garden gate. Of what else they conjure, I dinnae ken."

A small whirlwind of decaying forest debris spun into the
clearing on a gust of wind. In a billow of aged leaves, the
brownie appeared, landing on his rump in the dirt. He stood
and brushed dust from his clothing.

"What ken you of these matters, Munn?" Archie asked.

"Marcail of the pixie clan uses pixie dust to keep Gregor
enthralled."

"That cannot be true," Gregor said. "'Twas you who cast
a spell on my wine the night of my wedding."

With a shrug, Munn ignored the accusation. "And, the
pixie, Fenella, has done the same to Emily."

Emily gasped. Shocked by the revelation. She glared at
Archie. "Is that how you acquired my agreement for the
marriage?"

Munn gripped Tevin's hand. "Come with me lad, the
adults need time alone."

"I was unaware of any of these trickeries," Archie claimed.

"I don't want to be married anymore, especially not to
Gregor."

Gregor's pained gaze burned her. He opened his mouth as
if to say something, but Archie shook his head, and her

husband shut his mouth with a snap of his teeth.

"Before rash decisions are made, let me break the spells." Caitrina waved her arms over her head in graceful movements while swaying her hips and chanting syllables with lots of the *ch* sound. When strung together, the words sounded like what Emily would expect of an ancient language.

The air around Gregor wavered and blurred. He exhaled a puff of mist with a release of his breath. Their gazes met and held. She couldn't read his thoughts. Perhaps he felt disappointment. A moment later, she experienced the same phenomenon.

And, a kick of—regret.

Then her memory exploded...

"Oh, God! *Kim.*" Guilt swamped Emily. She crossed her arms over her chest and wrapped trembling hands over her sides in a tight self-hug. *How did I forget you, my love?* Tears burned the back of her eyes. She blinked them away. She refused to cry in front of all these people. To have her despair witnessed by Gregor.

Archie hustled the other warriors away, leaving Emily alone with Caitrina and Gregor.

"Kim would not wish you to go on mourning him," Caitrina whispered as she hugged Emily. "Do you want to go home, back to Anderson Creek, or do you wish to stay here in the past with Gregor?"

"Home I think. You can make that happen? Right?"

"Aye. I am a faerie with the ability to sift time."

Gregor approached somewhat hesitantly. "Your home is with me, lass."

"After all that has transpired?" Emily glanced to where the dead men had sprawled, but their bodies had been removed. She flicked her gaze back to Gregor "Everything between us was a lie."

He flinched. "Please. Stay with me. I love you."

Emily bit her lip. Isobell's words from the morning of the wedding sliced through her thoughts. Isobell had regretted allowing anger to blind her to Archie's love. And here, Emily was about to do the same with Gregor.

Did he really love her?

"Pixie dust cannot make you do something you dinnae want to do. It cannot override free will," Caitrina said. "The powder only makes a soul more open to possibilities."

How did Emily feel toward Gregor? Did she love him?

While she searched her mind and heart, at the edge of the woods, trees shifted and moved. A path opened. Caitrina guided them along the way to where vines were trembling. They moved of their own accord, slithering like snakes over a wall, unwrapping ancient gray stone, revealing a round gateway.

"This entrance to the nether was built by ancient *Sithicheans* and its magic will allow me to take you home. But you must hurry and decide, Emily, if you want to go back to Anderson Creek."

"We were not given a fair chance," Gregor said, his gaze imploring. "Please, find it in your heart to forgive me. Give us a second chance."

"Would you be willing to come to the future with me?"

"He cannot travel to the future, Emily." Caitrina shook her head. "His destiny is here in Scotland."

"Where is my destiny?"

"That is for you to decide."

Emily huffed out a long breath. Why was she the one required to leave behind the life she'd always known?

"If you decide to leave without me, I will find a way to come for you," Gregor said. "She is not the only faerie in Scotland."

"Dinnae be so disrespectful, lad," Caitrina scolded.

"I will not let you or anyone else come between us." Gregor glared at Caitrina.

Emily remembered Isobell's claim that Archie had come for her in their darkest moment, and that Gregor would always come for Emily. Could that be true?

Would he risk everything, his future in Scotland and

perhaps his life, to come for her? She didn't want him to do that. He had a good life here. Her life in Anderson Creek was rather dull. Life would be an adventure, here in Scotland with Gregor. Could she handle staying in the past?

While she hemmed and hawed, the faerie—Emily still had a hard time thinking of Caitrina as such—tapped a satin-slippered foot with impatience.

"Time runs short." Caitrina shoved Emily, and she hurled, face-first, through the stone gate.

"No," Gregor barked and grabbed her forearm before she completely disappeared. He yanked her back through the gate and into his arms. "I cannot let you go."

"I don't want to go." She twined her arms around his neck, and whisper kissed his lips. "I want to stay here with you. I love you."

"So be it." Caitrina didn't smile, but her lips quivered as if she fought the urge.

Munn returned with Tevin.

Caitrina glared at the brownie. "Stop using spelled wine. You always mess up the magic." She grasped the boy's hand. "Come, Tevin."

"I want to stay here with Emily," he whined.

"Don't you miss your mother and father?" Emily asked.

"Yeah, but I'll miss you and Gregor, too."

"We will think of you often, lad." Gregor ruffled the boy's hair the way Emily had a tendency to do.

"Okay," Tevin said. "I'll come back to visit Lach and hunt the orange dragon when I'm older. Tell Lach I said goodbye."

The faerie and the little boy stepped through the gate and vanished.

Emily leaned into Gregor's chest and kissed him hard on the mouth. His ardent response was a promise for their future together.

After the MacLachlan party buried the dead, mounted the horses, and rode homeward, Munn reappeared outside the cave. Marcail was where he suspected she'd be—inspecting the long-forgotten gateway to the nether Caitrina had exposed.

Munn's hands fisted at his sides and he glared at the pixie. "The queen will be displeased to learn you have meddled in the love affair of one of her favored Highlanders."

"Turned out for the best," Marcail said. "Besides, helping fated lovers find their way to each other works well for Caitrina. She is betrothed to Dugaid. The handsome *Prince of Darkness.*"

The leader of the pixie clan exhaled a long, audible sigh.

Munn rolled his eyes. "You dinnae ken of what you speak."

Marcail shrugged a delicate shoulder and flitted away as if without a care. As her flowery fae scent faded, a soft *tee teehee hee* whispered on the breeze.

Munn shook his head. One should never anger the Queen of the Fae. The foolish pixie remained unaware or uncaring of Oonagh's predilection for vengeance. 'Twas a hazardous place to be.

EPILOGUE

One year later
Castle Lachlan

*G*regor hurried through the courtyard and into the keep, taking the stairs to the great hall two at a time. While hunting today, he'd made a decision he wanted to share with his wife. He crossed the hall and headed for the back circular stair to the upper floors, expecting Emily to be in the ladies' solar.

Lady Isobell stopped him before he placed a foot on the first step. "I have a missive for you from Emily."

Her unnerving smile set him on edge. "Where is she?"

"Have nae fear all will be explained." The woman held out the note.

Why would he be presented with a missive if Emily was within the keep? After all this time had passed, had she decided to return to her future place? Without him? He accepted the note with an unsteady hand and quickly broke the seal.

The missive invited him to join Emily at the hunting lodge.

He raised a questioning gaze to Lady Isobell.

She shrugged a shoulder and strolled away to join her

husband and son near the hearth.

Gregor remained still for a moment, his mind whirring. *Ah! The she-devil.* A smile curved his lips, and he jumped into action, reversing his previous steps.

Anticipation chased him as he galloped across the large meadow, the stallion responsive to his eagerness. He reined the animal into the woodland trail and after making slower progress, arrived at the hunting lodge. Emily's mare contentedly munched from a bag of oats in the wattle and daub hut.

Gregor unsaddled his horse, set him to feed, and rubbed him down, while attempting to calm the frantic racing of his own heart.

He called out before opening the cottage door, wanting to reassure Emily he approached and not an intruder. She'd become quite proficient with her knives, and he preferred she not use the blades on him.

He stopped just past the threshold. The room glowed with candlelight. A feast fit for royalty had been spread upon the table. Emily, his beautiful wife, lay upon the furs atop the bed with naught covering her desirable body. The only feast he desired.

His arousal pressed hard against his trews.

"Hello, husband." The softly spoken greeting jerked him into action.

He crossed the floor with long strides. He marveled at her perfection. "Hello, wife."

She slid over and patted the mattress beside her.

He stripped quickly and joined her on the bed. "I went to find you at the castle, wanting to tell you of a decision I made. That is when Lady Isobell gave me your missive."

"I have something to share with you as well, but first, make love to me." Her husky voice and the desire in her soft blue eyes fired his blood and he couldn't deny the request.

Their loving flowed with beauty and intensity and, as always, like the first time.

Afterward, Emily caressed his chest, drawing wee circles

with nimble fingers.

"What is it, sweetling? What have you to tell me?"

"I'm going to have a baby...a *bairn*."

"You are?" The question near to strangled in his throat. At her tentative nod, he wrapped her in a tender embrace. "Your news has brought me immense joy."

"So, what was the decision you wanted to share with me?" Emily asked later while they ate.

"I have decided to nae longer stalk the white stag. I saw him today. He is a magnificent beast. He deserves to live a long life."

Emily squeezed his hand. "I'm glad."

Gregor no longer felt the need to prove himself to his father, to the chief, or to the clan. The only person's opinion that mattered to him was the love of his life—Emily.

Just His Fae Kiss

A Highland Gardens Novel
The 6th tale in the series.

Coming Soon
from
Dawn Marie Hamilton

Turn the page for a sneak peek…

CHAPTER ONE

Present day
Anderson Creek, North Carolina

"**S**he's been gone going on six years."

As if he didn't ken that fact. Douglas paced across the display floor of the *Celtic Image Shop*, his red and green MacKinnon kilt swaying with his stride, and flicked a glare at his business partner and best friend. That is, *if* someone like *him* could have a best friend. Five inches shorter than Douglas at six-foot-two and sporting one of the store's cream-colored logo t-shirts, Finn MacIntyre stood behind the checkout counter with a slight smirk curving his lips, blue eyes crinkled at the edges. Douglas ignored the urge to punch that damn golden-boy face.

An absolute contrast to Douglas's dark features. Darker mood.

Finn sobered; ran a hand through his honey-colored hair. "Where do you think she is?"

"Somewhere in Scotland, I presume." *Ancient Scotland.* Though he'd felt something change in the fabric of time. Was she on the move?

"Why don't you go after her?"

Finn's question stopped his pacing. "You dinnae understand. Caitrina is—"

"I know exactly *who* and *what* she is. Remember, she nefariously meddled in my life, that of my cousin's, and in countless others' amongst our friends."

"If you are referring to the matchmaking, it served you well."

"Perhaps, but Caitrina shouldn't have sent us to the past without our permission. She was in the wrong. Are you sure you want to stay involved with her?"

Douglas darkened his glower. Thunder rumbled over the mountains behind the shop.

"You always attract an excess of female attention at the Highland games," his buddy continued, ignoring the loud warning. "Since you're fond of redheads, why not date that singer from the Scottish tribal band you like? What's her name?"

"I *will* have Caitrina."

"Primitive attitude," Finn shot back.

More with the crashing of thunder and sky.

Finn sighed. "You've traveled to Scotland numerous times during the past six years. Why haven't you found her? Brought her back?"

"'Tis complicated."

"I'm sure it is."

"You are not helping."

The ringing of the wall phone stopped the discussion dead. Douglas met Finn's questioning glance. He gave an abrupt nod, and Finn picked up the receiver. "*Celtic Image Shop*. May I help you?" Finn's eyes flared. "What?" He grinned. "We'll be right over." He hung up the phone.

"What is it?" Douglas asked.

"Some news of which you'll be much interested." Finn's eyes glittered.

"Oh, stop with the suspense, will you?"

"Caitrina has returned with the missing Tevin."

Douglas's chest constricted. So that was why he'd been on

edge all day. But why had he not sensed her return? Had the effort to maintain the shopkeeper glamour for so long dimmed his power? The ramifications of such would be devastating.

"They are at Stephen and Jillian's house," Finn droned on. "It turns out some pixies lured the lad onto the faerie knoll just beyond the garden gate at *Foxgloves's* garden center and through the time gate. Emily got caught up in the magic and they both ended up at Castle Lachlan in sixteenth century Scotland. Archibald and Isobell took them in. So all is well that ends well."

"What of Emily?" Douglas finally managed to ask, even though he was more interested in Caitrina—his wayward faerie.

"Emily has decided to remain in Scotland past. Seems she married a MacLachlan warrior and is quite happy with him at Castle Lachlan."

Douglas tightened his jaw, his true self appalled by the twinge of guilt that gnawed at his gut. Still, as a man of the community, he should have gone back in time and seen to the protection of the wee lad and Emily after they were whisked away. He was the only one amongst the inhabitants of Anderson Creek possessing the ability to sift time at will.

Other than Caitrina, that is.

With her in hiding these many years, he hadn't believed she would get entangled with the manipulations of the mischievous Pixie Clan. Therefore, there had been no reason for him to get involved. Other than to be altruistic. Which his true self wasn't.

Of recent, the tug and pull of his duality tore at him relentlessly.

"Coming?" Finn dragged Douglas from his ping-ponging thoughts. "My pickup is out front."

"Nae. You go ahead. I need to close the shop. I will follow afterward in my truck." *But not as Douglas.*

"I can't thank you enough for bringing Tevin back to us."

Caitrina stiffened within Jillian's hug of gratitude, uncomfortable with the intense emotions flooding her psyche. One of which was guilt. If she had been watching over the clan, as she should have been, instead of sulking in the hills of ancient Scotland, fuming about her involuntary betrothal to the Dark Prince, the Pixie Clan never would have been so bold as to whisk Jillian's wee son, Tevin, and his babysitter, Emily, back through time.

Jillian kissed her cheek then returned to cuddling Tevin.

With hopes of quieting her mind, Caitrina stepped out of the crowded MacEwen log cabin and headed for *Foxglove's*, the garden center she owned with Jillian, and with Laurie MacLachlan. Aye, even hafling faerie princesses had human friends and business enterprises.

Garden clogs scuffing over the woodland trail, she took the short walk at a vigorous pace, glad she'd changed into a t-shirt and shorts. Perhaps she'd get her hands dirty puttering in the flower beds. That should make her feel better.

Only a few minutes passed before she entered through the front gate of the display garden and found the serenity she sought in the heady scents of an abundance of summer blooming plants. Bright pink *Stargazer* oriental lilies provided the most potent of the fragrances.

She dropped onto the stone garden bench with an audible sigh. The joyous reunion of Tevin with his parents and the exuberant well-wishers had brought on a mind-numbing melancholy along with the guilt. She'd missed her friends during the six year self-imposed banishment.

All their friends from Anderson Creek were at the house to celebrate Tevin's return. Except for one. Why hadn't Douglas come?

He claimed to be in love with Caitrina. Okay, that was six years ago. Had he lost interest during her absence? Had he found someone new? Married?

Finn claimed to have informed him of her return. Said Douglas planned to drive over in his truck. But several hours had passed and the man was a no show.

Damn the man. She'd missed him terribly while she'd been gone.

Caitrina's sensitive ears perked at a nearby rustle of leaves. Someone approached from the rear of the garden. Someone who smelled very much like a faerie. A familiar faerie. *Shite!* Caitrina jumped to her feet. Darted a panicked gaze from side to side. Thought to fade into the vanishing. *Shite, shite, shite!* She wasn't calm enough to disappear.

She needed to slow her heart rate. Concentrate. But how could she do that when she'd been thinking of Douglas. And now this…

Stop it. She shouldn't be so fretful. *He* wouldn't come to her on foot. Her betrothed wouldn't lower himself to such a human mode of mobility. He would just appear in front of her from the nether and issue unreasonable demands.

To prove her wrong, Dugaid strode from the rhododendron trail in all his dark, masculine beauty, the black silk mask covering a portion of his face adding to his raw sex appeal. Garbed in black leather, and with all manner of weaponry draping his powerful six-foot seven frame, no one could mistake him for any other than the Prince of the Black River. The Son of the King and Queen of the Fae. The Dark Prince. Caitrina's betrothed.

Mouth agape, she stepped back and bumped against the bench.

"Dinnae try to escape me, princess. 'Tis pointless." His dark voice…excited her. Her nipples pebbled and her sex wept. Dammit to hell! He stopped in front of her, infringing on her personal space. His captivating fae scent, the elemental smell of a violent storm, overpowered the fragrance of the garden, enticing her to melt at his feet.

Caitrina reached up to touch his silky black hair, but stayed her hand.

She must fight this inconvenient attraction. It was a betrayal of her love for Douglas.

Dugaid's bulk loomed over her. Intimidated her. She

stiffened her spine, raised her chin, looked through the slits in the mask, and into his challenging tiger-like gaze. His distinctive yellow eyes with black pupils flared.

"Why are you here?" she asked, although she kenned the reason.

"To collect what belongs to me."

"I have naught of yours," she countered.

He laughed. "Oh, but you do. You have everything I desire, my love."

His large hand snaked out and encircled her wrist, thumb slowly circling over her racing pulse. He attempted to tame her? She couldn't summon the vanishing. Panic burned in her belly. She was trapped.

"Let. Go. Of. Me," she gritted, voice rising to punctuate each word.

"Never." His grasp tightened.

"Take your hand off her." A foolishly brave Finn MacIntyre stood several feet away with naught but a small hunting knife in his hand.

"In time, you will come to me willingly, *my love*," Dugaid whispered near her ear. He inhaled sharply, as if breathing in her very essence. "Until we meet again."

With a brusque motion, he released his grip and turned to Finn. "I mean her nae harm."

Then Dugaid faded into the vanishing.

"Who the hell was that? One of your kind?" Finn strode forward.

"Aye." Caitrina gave a curt nod.

Angry lightning zigzagged across an ominous sky. Thunder roared. The smell of ozone tinged the air.

Finn glanced up. Lines furrowed his forehead. "Sounds like we're in for one hell of a storm."

An understatement, if ever she'd heard one. Caitrina sank to the garden bench. She refused to shed a tear in front of Finn.

Dammit to hell. How was she to get out of the betrothal?

ALSO BY DAWN MARIE HAMILTON

Just Beyond the Garden Gate
A Highland Gardens Novel
The first tale in the time travel fantasy series

Just Once in a Verra Blue Moon
A Highland Gardens Novel
The second tale in the time travel fantasy series

Just in Time for a Highland Christmas
A Highland Gardens Novella
The third tale in the time travel fantasy series

Just Wait For Me
A Highland Gardens Novel
The fourth tale in the time travel fantasy series

Twelvetide
Twelve Nights of Highland Magic
An Enchanted Highlands Novella

Sea Panther
A Crimson Storm Novel
The first book in the paranormal series

Twelvetide
Twelve Nights of Highland Magic
An Enchanted Highlands Holiday Novella

by Dawn Marie Hamilton

Time Travel Romance

He has twelve nights to gain her love.
She has twelve nights to save his soul.

Fulfilling a childhood promise, Ashley Dumont returns to an ancient Druid garden in the Black Hills of Scotland on the eve of the winter solstice—a time when magic hums and the veil between realms thins and tears, allowing all manner of supernatural creatures through. Will the ghost who claimed to be her destiny still be there?

Caelan Innes awaits her arrival. Unjustly murdered in the sixteenth century, a second chance at life depends on this woman. The Druids grant them the twelve nights of Yule to find love and save Cael's soul. Will a trip through time and the treachery of enemies make the sacrifice too dear?

Sea Panther
A Crimson Storm Series Novel

by Dawn Marie Hamilton

Paranormal Romance

2013 Golden Heart® finalist for Best Paranormal Romance

Can love mend a fractured soul?

After evading arrest for Jacobite activities, Scottish nobleman Robert MacLachlan turns privateer. A Caribbean Voodoo priestess curses him to an eternal existence as a vampire shifter torn between the dual natures of a Florida panther and an immortal blood-thirsting man. For centuries, he seeks to reverse the black magic whilst maintaining his honor. Cruising the twenty-first century Atlantic, he becomes shorthanded to sail his 90-foot yacht, *Sea Panther*. The last thing he wants is a female crewmember and the call of her blood.

Although she swore never to sail again after her father died in a sailing accident, Kimberly Scot answers the captain's crew wanted ad to escape a hit man. She's lost everything, her fiancé, her job, and most of her money, along with money belonging to her ex-clients. A taste of Kimberly's blood convinces Robert she is the one woman who can claim the panther's heart. To break the curse, they travel back in time to where it all began—Jamaica 1715.

FUTURE WORKS:

Time Travel Fantasy Romance

Just His Fae Kiss
Highland Gardens Series Novel

Paranormal Romance

Raven's Revenge
Crimson Storm Series Novel

Jagger's Justice
Crimson Storm Series Novel

Dear Readers,

Thank you for reading *Just Within a Highland Mist!* I hope you enjoyed Emily and Gregor's tale.

If you love time travel romance, consider joining the **Hearts Trough Time** closed Facebook group and/or Website where myself and several other time travel romance authors gather with readers to discuss our favorite genre—time travel romance.

Join the discussions at:

Facebook: www.facebook.com/groups/heartsthroughtime
Website: www.heartsthroughtime.com

Hope to greet you there.

~Dawn Marie

ABOUT THE AUTHOR

Dawn Marie Hamilton dares you to dream. She is a 2013 RWA® Golden Heart® Finalist who pens Scottish-inspired fantasy and paranormal romance. Some of her tales are rife with mischief-making faeries, brownies, and other fae creatures. More tormented souls—shape shifters, vampires, and maybe a zombie or two—stalk across the pages of other stories. When not writing, she's cooking, gardening, or paddling the local creeks with her husband.

Visit Dawn Marie on the web at:
dawnmariehamilton.blogspot.com
facebook.com/authorDawnMarieHamilton

www.ingramcontent.com/pod-product-compliance
Lightning Source LLC
Chambersburg PA
CBHW030543130626
46552CB00006B/2400